Art Fiction Stories

II

Art Fiction Stories
II

Edited by Ellen Francese

PP

Portmay Press
New York

All images courtesy of the Metropolitan Museum of Art's Open Access initiative

Cover image: El Greco (Domenikos Theotokopoulos), *View of Toledo* (ca. 1599–1600), The Metropolitan Museum of Art, New York, H. O. Havemeyer Collection, Bequest of Mrs. H. O. Havemeyer, 1929

Project management and design by Emily Albarillo

Printed in the United States of America
First published in 2022 by Portmay Press, New York

Library of Congress Control Number: 2022903939

ISBN 978-1-7360536-5-2 (pb)
ISBN 978-1-7360536-6-9 (ebook)

PP
Portmay Press
244 Madison Avenue
New York, NY 10016
www.portmaypress.com

Art Fiction Stories II *is the second in an innovative series of collected works of art fiction. Each story in this volume was chosen for the unique way in which the author paints with words and, whether from the perspective of the nineteenth century, the twentieth, or the twenty-first, embraces the intersections of art, life, and fiction. Each story has been paired with a painting from the Metropolitan Museum of Art and is preceded by a reflection by Ellen Francese exploring the connections between the story and the work of art.*

Daffodils
ELIZABETH BOWEN

and

Geraldine Russell
JOHN WHITE ALEXANDER

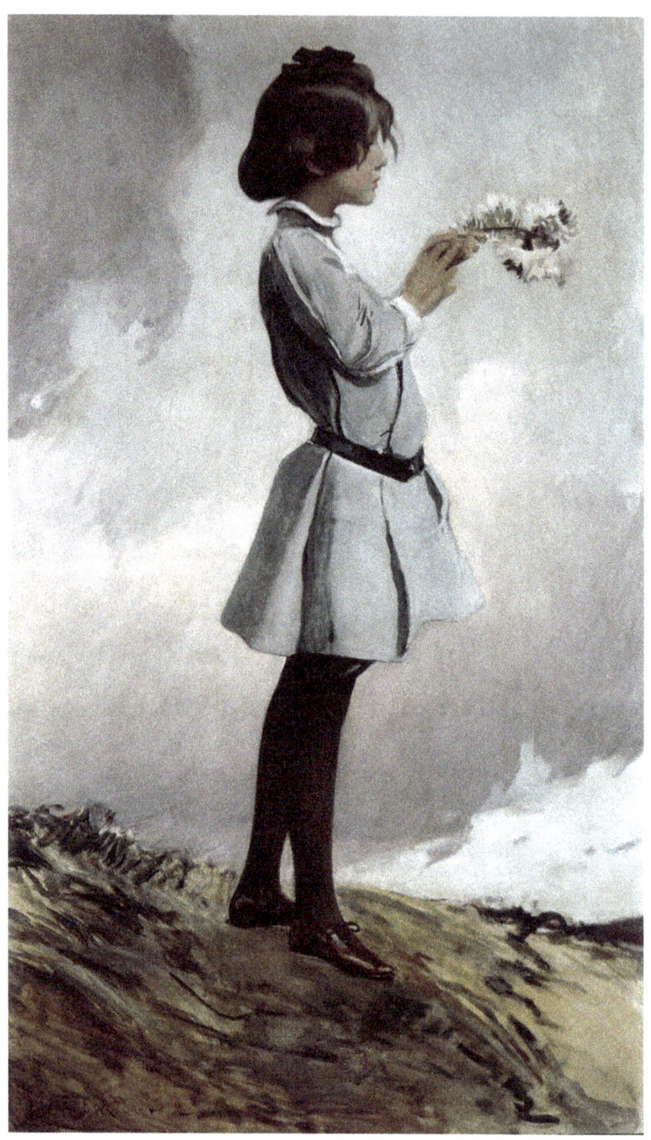

John White Alexander, *Geraldine Russell* (1902 or 1903), Gift of Charles H. Russell, 1964.

Artists have always known that Nature offers joy, beauty, and instruction. Children recognize this freely and instinctively. It is often school and adulthood that narrow their vision and loosen their connection with the natural world. John White Alexander's painting *Geraldine Russell* offers us an opportunity to witness a young girl who stands at the border of carefree childhood and the isolated gray expanse of her unknown future. Her slender, curved body balances against the forward droop of the daffodil sprig held by both her hands. Her dull, blue-gray frock echoes the colors of the stormy sky that swirl around her. The white daffodils offer no sunshine. The only warmth we see is the faint, rosy blush of her cheeks. Solemnly, she stands, seemingly turned inward against the barren landscape and sky. Her clothes belie her youth: her belt disallows the flow of fabric, so no amount of dancing can elicit a joyful billowing, and her narrow, polished shoes point to a colorless life of stern, fashionable existence. This portrait of Geraldine Russell provides a context in which to explore Elizabeth Bowen's "Daffodils." Miss Murcheson seeks to awaken somehow the dull world around her by teaching her resistant, adolescent students to think and feel deeply. We first meet her as she buys and clutches the daffodil bouquet. As the wind lifts her skirts, she tries to maintain her decorum. The reader alone sees that no one has noticed. The protagonist is thus set apart from the city around her. She revels in the coming spring, echoing the Wordsworth poem fragment of daffodils "dancing in the breeze." Her belief that something marvelous is coming is set against the closed-faced, gated houses where only a stray, budding branch can slip through to touch her. It seems that the unnatural, bright light is there to remind us to observe her at a distance. When we enter her dark home, we feel her misgivings from the leftover, dense smell of food and the feeling of emptiness in the insistent shadows. Even her familiar sitting room seems foreign to her when the girls enter and change her context. Her teacher's lens will not work here. The girls saturate the room with their color, blossoming bodies, and energy. The old photograph of their teacher reveals a presence that attracts the girls, something not quite recognized by Miss Murcheson, who cannot open up to passionately loving another. As we witness this meeting of youth and adulthood, we recall the fragment of Herrick's poem "Daffodils," where we follow our quick blossoming and decay in this world. How do we live a full, present life? We are left with the contrast between an isolated, yearning teacher and a group of strolling teens, framed by a window. Is it possible to look within ourselves for the answers? Our eyes return to the painting of Geraldine Russell which perpetually asks this question.

—Ellen Francese

Daffodils

Elizabeth Bowen

First published in 1923 in Encounters *by Boni and Liveright .*

Miss Murcheson stopped at the corner of the High Street to buy a bunch of daffodils from the flower-man. She counted out her money very carefully, pouring a little stream of coppers from her purse into the palm of her hand.

"—ninepence—ten—eleven—pence half-penny—a *shilling*! Thank you very much. Good afternoon."

A gust of wind rushed up the street, whirling her skirts up round her like a ballet-dancer's, and rustling the Reckitts-blue paper round the daffodils. The slender gold trumpets tapped and quivered against her face as she held them up with one hand and pressed her skirts down hastily with the other. She felt as though she had been enticed into a harlequinade by a company of Columbines who were quivering with laughter at her discomfiture; and looked round to see if anyone had witnessed her display of chequered moirette petticoat and the inches of black stocking above her boots. But the world remained unembarrassed.

To-day the houses seemed taller and farther apart; the street wider and full of a bright, clear light that cast no shadows and was never sunshine. Under archways and between the houses the distances had a curious transparency, as though they had been painted upon glass. Against the luminous and indeterminate sky the Abbey tower rose distinct and delicate.

Miss Murcheson, forgetting all confusion, was conscious of her wings. She paused again to hitch up the bundle of exercise books slithering down beneath her elbow, then took the dipping road as a bird swings down into the air. Her mouth was faintly acrid with spring dust and the scent of daffodils was in her nostrils. As she left the High Street further behind her, the traffic sounded as a faint and murmurous hum, striking here and there a tinkling note like wind-bells.

Under her detachment she was conscious of the houses, the houses and the houses. They were square, flat-faced and plaster-fronted, painted creams and greys and buffs; one, a purplish rose colour. Venetian shutters flat against the wall broadened the line of the windows, there were coloured fanlights over all the doors. Spiked railings before them shut off their little squares of grass or gravel from the road, and between the railings branches swung out to brush against her dress and recall her to the wonder of their budding loveliness.

Miss Murcheson remembered that her mother would be out for tea, and quickened her steps in anticipation of that delightful solitude. The silver birch tree that distinguished their front garden slanted beckoning her across the pavement. She hesitated, as her gate swung open, and stood looking up and down the road. She was sorry to go in, but could not resist the invitation of the empty house. She wondered if to-morrow would fill her with so strange a stirring as to-day. Soon, in a few months, it would be summer and there would be nothing more to come. Summer would be beautiful, but this spring made promise of a greater beauty than summer could fulfil; hinted at a mystery which other summers had evaded rather than explained. She went slowly up the steps, fumbling for her latch-key.

The day's dinner still hung dank and heavy in the air of the little hall. She stood in the doorway, with that square of light and sound behind her, craving the protection and the comfort with which that dark entrance had so often received her. There was a sudden desolation in the emptiness of the house.

Quickly she entered the sitting-room and flung open the window, which set the muslin curtains swaying in the breeze and clanked the little pictures on the walls. The window embrasure was so deep that there was little light in the corners of the room; armchairs and cabinets were lurking in the dusk. The square of daylight by the window was blocked by a bamboo table groaning under an array of photographs.

In her sweeping mood she deposed the photographs, thrust the table to one side, and pulled her chair up into the window. "I can't correct my essays in the dark," she asserted, though she had done so every evening of the year.

"How tight-laced you are, poor Columbines," she said, throwing away the paper and seeing how the bass cut deep into the fleshy stems. "You were brave above it all, but—there now!" She cut the bass and shook the flowers out into a vase. "I can't correct," she sighed, "with you all watching me. You are so terribly flippant!"

But what a curious coincidence: she had set her class to write an essay upon Daffodils! "You shall judge; I'll read them all out loud. They *will* amuse you." She dipped her pen in the red-ink pot with an anticipatory titter.

With a creak of wheels a young woman went by slowly, wheeling a perambulator. She leant heavily on the handle-bar, tilting the perambulator on its two back wheels, and staring up, wide-mouthed, at the windows.

"How nice to be so much interested," thought Miss Murcheson, pressing open the first exercise-book. "But I'm sure it can't be a good thing for the baby."

The essays lacked originality. Each paragraph sidled up self-consciously to openings for a suitable quotation, to rush each one through with a gasp of triumph.

"And then my heart with pleasure fills
And dances with the daffodils."

"Fair daffodils, we weep to see
You fade away so soon."

She wondered if any of her class could weep for the

departure of a daffodil. Mostly they had disclaimed responsibility for such weakness by the stern prefix, "As the poet says———." Flora Hopwood had, she remembered, introduced a "Quotation Dictionary," which must have been the round of her circle.

"I must forbid it. Why can't they see things for themselves, think them out? I don't believe they ever really see anything, just accept things on the authority of other people. I could make them believe anything. What a responsibility teaching is——— But is it? They'd believe me, but they wouldn't care. It wouldn't matter, really.

"They're so horribly used to things. Nothing ever comes new to them that they haven't grown up with. They get their very feelings out of books. Nothing ever surprises or impresses them. When spring comes they get preoccupied, stare dreamily out of the windows. They're thinking out their new hats. Oh, if only I didn't know them quite so well, or knew them a little better!

"If I had a school of my own," she meditated, running her eyes down the pages and mechanically underlining spelling-mistakes, "I would make them think. I'd horrify them, if nothing better. But here—how ever can one, teaching at a High School? Miss Peterson would———

"They *do* like me. At least, one set does, I know. I'm rather a cult, they appreciate my Titian hair. They'd like me more, though, if I knew how to do it better, and knew better how to use my eyes. Their sentimentality embarrasses me. In a way they're so horribly mature, I feel at a disadvantage with them. If only they'd be a little more spontaneous.

But spontaneity is beyond them at present. They're simply calves, after all, rather sophisticated calves."

She dreamed, and was awakened by familiar laughter. Nobody's laughter in particular, but surely it was the laughter of the High School? Three girls were passing with arms close linked, along the pavement underneath her window. She looked down on the expressive, tilted ovals of their sailor hats; then, on an impulse, smacked the window-sill to attract their attention. Instantly they turned up three pink faces of surprise, which broadened into smiles of recognition.

"Hullo, Miss Murcheson!"

"Hullo, children! Come in for a minute and talk to me. I'm all alone."

Millicent, Rosemary and Doris hesitated, eyeing one another, poised for flight. "Righto!" they agreed unanimously.

Miss Murcheson, all of a flutter, went round to open the front door. She looked back at the sitting-room as though she had never seen it before.

Why had she asked them in, those terrible girls whom she had scarcely spoken to? They would laugh at her, they would tell the others.

The room was full of them, of their curiosity and embarrassment and furtive laughter. She had never realised what large girls they were; how plump and well-developed. She felt them eyeing her stack of outraged relatives, the photographs she swept off on to a chair; their eyes flitted from the photographs to the daffodils, from the daffodils to the open, red-scored exercise books.

"Yes," she said, "your writings, I daresay. Do you

recognise them? I was correcting 'Daffodils' and they made me dreary—sit down, won't you?—*dreary*. I wonder if any of you have ever used your senses; smelt, or *seen* things——— Oh, *do* sit down!"

She seemed to be shouting into a forest of thick bodies. They seated themselves along the edge of an ottoman in a bewildered row; this travestied their position in the classroom and made her feel, facing them, terribly official and instructive. She tried to shake this off.

"It's cruel, isn't it, to lie in wait for you like this and pull you in and lecture you about what you don't feel about daffodils!"

Her nervous laughter tinkled out into silence.

"It was a beastly subject," said someone, heavily.

"Beastly? Oh, Mill—Rosemary, have you never seen a daffodil?"

They giggled.

"No, but looked at one?" Her earnestness swept aside her embarrassment. "Not just heard about them—'Oh yes, daffodils: yellow flowers; spring, mother's vases, bulbs, borders, flashing past flower-shop windows'—but taken one up in your hands and felt it?"

How she was haranguing them!

"It's very difficult to be clever about things one's *used* to," said Millicent. "That's why history essays are so much easier. You tell us about things, and we just write them down."

"That's why you're so lazy; you're using *my* brains; just giving me back what I gave you again, a little bit the worse for the wear."

They looked hurt and uncomfortable.

Doris got up and walked over to the fire-place.

("Good," thought Miss Murcheson, "it will relieve the tension a bit if they will only begin to prowl.")

"What a pretty photograph. Miss Murcheson. Who is it? Not—not *you*?"

"*Me*?" said Miss Murcheson with amusement. "Yes. Why not? Does it surprise you, then?"

"You've got such a *dinky* hat on!" cried the girl, with naive astonishment.

The others crowded round her.

"You look so different," said Doris, still scrutinising the photograph. "Awfully happy, and prosperous, and—cocksure."

"Perhaps it was the hat!" suggested Millicent.

"Oh, *Millicent*! No, I'm sure Miss Murcheson was *thinking* about something nice."

"Or somebody."

"Oh, Doris, you are awful!"

They all giggled, and glanced apprehensively across at her.

She wondered why she was not more offended by them.

"As a matter of fact," she enlightened them, "*that* was because of daffodils. It just illustrates my point, curiously enough."

They were still absorbed.

"Oh, Miss *Murcheson*!"

"*Miss* Murcheson!"

"When was it taken?"

"Last Easter holidays. Nearly a year ago. At Seabrooke. By a friend of mine."

"*Do-oo* give me one!"

"———And me?"

"I'm afraid that's the only print I've got; and that's mother's."

"Were there more?"

"Yes, various people took them. You see, I haven't faced a real camera for years, so when I got these snaps they were scrambled for by people who'd been asking me for photos."

"People?" She was rising visibly in their estimation.

"Oh yes. Friends."

"Why *daffodils*?" reverted Rosemary.

"Somebody had just given me a great big bunch." She was impressed by their interest. "I wonder if daffodils will ever make any of you look like that."

"It all depends, you see," said Millicent, astutely. "Nobody has ever given us any. If they *did* perhaps———"

"*Really*?" said Miss Murcheson, with innocent concern. "Take all those, if they would really inspire you! No, dears, I'd *like* you to."

She gathered the daffodils together and lifted them, dripping, from the vase.

The girls retreated.

"Oh no, really, *not* your daffodils———"

"We don't mean———"

"Not *your* daffodils. Miss Murcheson. It wasn't *that* a bit."

Evidently a false move on her part. She was bewildered

by them; could not fathom the depths of their cinema-bred romanticism.

Doris had put away the photograph and stood with her back to the others, fingering the ornaments on the chimney-piece.

"There are lots of things," she said rapidly, "that you only feel because of people. That's the only reason things are there for, I *think*. You wouldn't notice them otherwise, or care about them. It's only sort of———" She stopped. Her ears glowed crimson underneath her hat.

"Association," they sighed, ponderously.

"That's exactly what's the matter," cried Miss Murcheson. "We've got all the nice, fresh, independent, outside things so smeared over with our sentimentalities and prejudices and—associations—that we can't see them anyhow but as part of ourselves. That's how you're—we're missing things and spoiling things for ourselves. You—we don't seem able to *discover*."

"Life," said Doris sententiously, "is a very big adventure. Of course we all see *that*."

The other two looked at her quickly. All three became suddenly hostile. She was encouraging them to outrage the decencies of conversation. It was bad form, this flagrant discussion of subjects only for their most secret and fervid whisperings.

To her, they were still unaccountable. She had not wished to probe.

"I don't think that's what I meant," she said a little flatly.

"Of course your lives will be full of interesting things, and those will be your own affairs. Only, if I could be able, I'm always trying, to make you care about the little fine things you might pass over, that have such big roots underground.

"I should like you to be as happy as I've been, and as I'm going to be," she said impulsively. "I should love to watch you after you've left my form, going up and up the school, and getting bigger, and then, when you've left, going straight and clearly to the essential things."

The tassel of the blind cord tapped against the window-sill, through the rustling curtains they looked out on to the road.

They had awaited a disclosure intimate and personal. The donor of those last year's daffodils had taken form, portentous in their minds. But she had told them nothing, given them the stone of her abstract, colourless idealism while they sat there, open-mouthed for sentimental bread.

"Won't you stay to tea?" she asked. "Oh, *do*. We'll picnic; boil the kettle on the gas-ring, and eat sticky buns—I've got a bag of sticky buns. We'll have a party in honour of the daffodils."

The prospect allured her, it would be a fantastic interlude.

They all got up.

"Doris and Millicent are coming to tea with me, Miss Murcheson. Mother's expecting us, thanks most awfully. Else we should have loved to."

"We should have loved to," echoed the others. "Thanks most awfully."

She felt a poignant disappointment and relief, as standing with her eyes on the daffodils, she heard the children clattering down the steps.

To-morrow they will be again impersonal; three pink moons in a firmament of faces.

The three, released, eyed one another with a common understanding.

"Miss Murcheson has never really *lived*," said Doris.

They linked arms again and sauntered down the road.

Autumn Whorl

MARYANN D'AGINCOURT

and

Autumn Landscape

XIANG SHENGMO

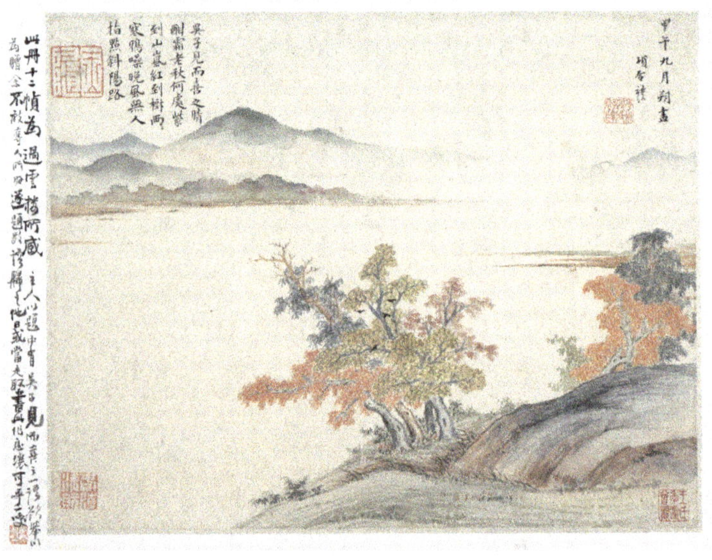

Xiang Shengmo, *Autumn Landscape* (1654), Seymour Fund, 1964.

Our relationship with Nature's landscape is defined by culture, both individual and collective. Depending on our lens, we may see ourselves as dominating, insignificant, or equal. Visual artists explore these relationships. Over a thirty-year span, Paul Cézanne sought to conquer Mont Sainte Victoire by painting it from multiple perspectives. The Japanese artist Katsushika Hokusai's print series Thirty-Six Views of Mount Fuji always lures the eyes to the mountain instead of lingering with other natural elements or the rare people placed on the landscape. Native Americans have traditionally abstracted Nature, reminding us of its multiple powers, and have fundamentally defined us as a part of the landscape rather than as an external viewer. Xiang Shengmo's *Autumn Landscape* offers us the magnificent sweep of land and water that is distilled in muted cool and warm hues. Our gaze travels the distance between each shore from the trees to the mountains. Rather than feel diminished by the landscape, we are caught in the absolute stillness, perhaps emptiness, before us, which tempers distance and size, crystallizing this moment. What Shengmo explores through space as a painter, Maryann D'Agincourt examines through the temporal narrative and its relationship to Nature in "Autumn Whorl." We are not given a time reference, though we understand that this story has already taken place. Despite the time gap, the narrative reads as if the event is happening now. The fiery leaves ignite in the sun as the narrator, Jocelyn, walks from school to a home that has been shifting its identity since her father has been mostly absent. We understand the duality of growth as Jocelyn notes both her mother's newly found commitment to her art studies which divides her from her daughter and her increased tenderness which binds. The unexpected scene of her mother's posing beneath the red maple surrounded by leaves ablaze for Jocelyn's art teacher embodies her mother's claim for independence. Her daughter, however, feels the panic of female vulnerability, later yielding to a terror and despair. Her experience has shifted the physical landscape, moving the tree to the foreground with vivid detail, kindling her own isolation and fear. The magnified scene enfolds her, even as she hides beneath her bed's covers and presses her hands over her ears. Jocelyn's rite of passage violently arouses within her the desire to return to her childhood, rolling in the colorful, benign leaves of autumn. Her acute loneliness brings us back to the silent, open space of Shengmo's landscape.

—Ellen Francese

Autumn Whorl

Maryann D'Agincourt

First published in Able Muse *in 2010.*

In the afternoon sun, fallen leaves moist from a soft morning rainfall were strewn across the sidewalk like embers. It was a breezy October day. On my way home from school, pressing my homework folder to my chest to protect the sheets inside from the wind, I half wondered if my mother would be home. Because of his work the past few months, my father had to be in New York on weekdays. In his absence it was as if our house suddenly had a large hole in the center and my mother and I both had to walk gingerly around its periphery. We were surprised, as we hadn't realized how much of a part he played in holding the three of us together. So we occupied ourselves with other things, things that led us away from that dark, unseen hole.

Mother enrolled in a course in art history at the museum, a seminar on Rembrandt, and said she would apply for graduate credit. She studied more now, and I'd often find her in the middle of the night in the small study at the back of our home, wrapped in her green velvet bathrobe, hunched over the typewriter, punching the keys. She'd be sleepy but determined, a half-filled cup of tea rattling on her desk. I'd stand behind her and watch. She wouldn't turn her head; she'd just keep typing. After a while she'd stop, then lift her chin. Clacking a red-painted fingernail against one key, she'd say, "Jocelyn, honey, it's time now to go to bed." I'd tiptoe out of the room, and she wouldn't resume typing until I was halfway down the hall. My mother put her whole self into writing. When she held one of the papers she'd been working on in her hand, it was as if it was a part of her body, another limb.

Lately I'd begun to see a change in her; she was less critical than when my father was at home, less questioning of my whereabouts, but at the same time she was more affectionate toward me, more so than she'd been in the past.

Because she'd been spending more and more time at the library and wasn't certain how long she'd need to study on a particular day, she'd given me a key to let myself in. When I reached the house that day, I rang the bell and waited. She wasn't home. I pulled out the key from my skirt pocket and opened the door. Soon I went into the study to do to my homework. I found Mother's papers scattered across the top of the desk. Because the blinds of the single window that faced the backyard were closed, the title of the paper was difficult to read.

I had a math assignment, some word problems to work on, and I needed more light to see the numbers on the sheet. Before I sat down, I put my mother's papers in the top drawer of the desk and then pulled open the venetian blinds. The strong autumn light filled the room. From where I stood I could see the entire backyard—and there under the maple tree sat my mother, among the deep-red leaves on the ground. Her ankles and feet were hidden beneath her dark green billowy skirt; the buttons on her burgundy blouse were undone. At that moment a strong breeze blew, opening her shirt, fully revealing her small breasts. I stuck my fist inside my mouth to prevent myself from crying out—she was not alone. My art teacher, wearing the same gray pants and white shirt he'd had on in class that day, stood a few feet away from her holding a large pad of paper in one hand with a low-burning cigarette between two fingers. His other hand moved quickly across the sheet. He sketched freely, unmoved by the sight of my mother's breasts. With his head lowered to the paper in concentration, his expression was earnest, absorbed, his dark shiny hair falling across his forehead. I yanked the window cord with my free hand and the blinds snapped shut. Then I ran upstairs to my bedroom, locked the door, and got into bed and under the covers. As I lay there I kept replaying in my mind my mother's calm, steady expression, her small breasts, the art teacher's impartial, sweeping glance, the quick movement of his hand as he sketched. And at that moment I wished the maple tree had not been so close, so easy to see from where I stood. It was as if I was looking through binoculars, and my mother and he were unnaturally close to me, every detail of their beings exposed, enlarged by the strong lenses. Though my mind was racing and my heart thumping beyond control, I remained quiet and still beneath the covers, fearful that any movement on my part would draw attention to my whereabouts.

Soon I heard the back door open, and then the sound of their footsteps in the kitchen, their voices low, weary sounding. I blocked my ears; I didn't want to listen to their words. I lay in bed with my eyes tightly closed, imagined my mother insisting that he stay, her expression pleading, her hair falling down past her shoulders, her blouse open. I pressed my hands even more firmly against my ears and held still in this position, yearning to roll in the leaves.

False Dawn
EDITH WHARTON

and

Corridor in the Asylum
VINCENT VAN GOGH

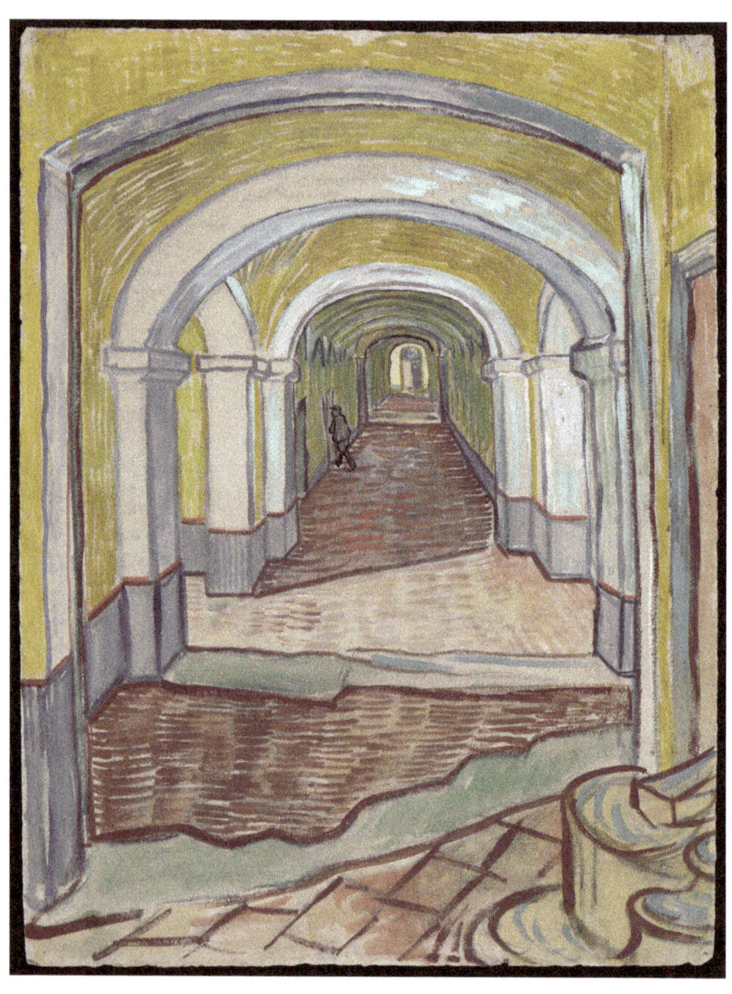

Vincent Van Gogh, *Corridor in the Asylum* (September 1889), Bequest of Abby Aldrich Rockefeller, 1948.

While Nature follows through each day by offering us another sunrise that cracks open night's darkness, presenting us with new possibilities, what we may hope for often breaks or burns off like early morning fog. Life, like architecture, is a construct that we build. Too often we fortify it with the belief that we will be invincible. Our own hubris blinds us to the widening fissures. The ones we may notice, we may explain in a way that sustains our narratives or allows us to create a new path. Vincent Van Gogh's painting *Corridor in the Asylum* unfolds an interior view which pulls us into an endless hall framed by arches that flank unseen, uncountable, diverging corridors. The dull colors offer no hope: sickly sulfur yellow, anemic green, graying blue, and dried-blood red. At a distance we can see a small, solitary dark figure entering a hidden hallway. The heaviness of the architectural style bears down on us, only increasing the feeling of emptiness and loneliness. Perhaps once this building served a happier purpose, but no longer. We cannot imagine the possibility of creating well-being here. Van Gogh's illusion of his own healing belied his deep despair as his suicide quickly followed his release from the asylum. In Edith Wharton's story "False Dawn," Halston Raycie has obscured a piece of American history by brazenly building his Long Island Tuscan villa, a testimony to his enduring status within New York's wealthy society. Later, his desire to increase his rank drives him to plan to recreate part of his city residence into a prestigious art gallery. He has always controlled the details of his life and his family, from the allocation of money to the details of food and dress. The absolutism of his expectations seems unbreakable. Only in the predawn darkness do we see his daughter Mary Adeline and son Lewis live out choices that undermine their father's blueprint. The story follows Lewis's awakening in Europe, a rite of passage that defies his father's narrow directive. The transformed eyes with which Lewis sees the world more deeply connect him to the faithful, saint-like girl he temporarily left behind and sever him forever from his father. Even though Lewis's new vision, embodied in the art gallery housed in Cousin Ebenezer's worn-down former residence, offers a false hope for the immediate present, his dream will be validated after his death. No matter the strength and beauty of our architecture, we will at times face deserted, dreary halls. It is up to us how we manage them.

—Ellen Francese

False Dawn

Edith Wharton

First published in 1924 in Old New York *by D. Appleton and Company.*

I

Hay, verbena and mignonette scented the languid July day. Large strawberries, crimsoning through sprigs of mint, floated in a bowl of pale yellow cup on the verandah table: an old Georgian bowl, with complex reflections on polygonal flanks, engraved with the Raycie arms between lions' heads. Now and again the gentlemen, warned by a menacing hum, slapped their cheeks, their brows or their bald crowns; but they did so as furtively as possible, for

Mr. Halston Raycie, on whose verandah they sat, would not admit that there were mosquitoes at High Point.

The strawberries came from Mr. Raycie's kitchen garden; the Georgian bowl came from his great-grandfather (father of the Signer); the verandah was that of his country-house, which stood on a height above the Sound, at a convenient driving distance from his town house in Canal Street.

"Another glass, Commodore," said Mr. Raycie, shaking out a cambric handkerchief the size of a table-cloth, and applying a corner of it to his steaming brow.

Mr. Jameson Ledgely smiled and took another glass. He was known as "the Commodore" among his intimates because of having been in the Navy in his youth, and having taken part, as a midshipman under Admiral Porter, in the war of 1812. This jolly sunburnt bachelor, whose face resembled that of one of the bronze idols he might have brought back with him, had kept his naval air, though long retired from the service; and his white duck trousers, his gold-braided cap and shining teeth, still made him look as if he might be in command of a frigate. Instead of that, he had just sailed over a party of friends from his own place on the Long Island shore; and his trim white sloop was now lying in the bay below the point.

The Halston Raycie house overlooked a lawn sloping to the Sound. The lawn was Mr. Raycie's pride: it was mown with a scythe once a fortnight, and rolled in the spring by an old white horse specially shod for the purpose. Below the verandah the turf was broken by three round beds of rose-geranium, heliotrope and Bengal roses, which Mrs.

Raycie tended in gauntlet gloves, under a small hinged sunshade that folded back on its carved ivory handle. The house, remodelled and enlarged by Mr. Raycie on his marriage, had played a part in the Revolutionary war as the settler's cottage where Benedict Arnold had had his headquarters. A contemporary print of it hung in Mr. Raycie's study; but no one could have detected the humble outline of the old house in the majestic stone-coloured dwelling built of tongued-and-grooved boards, with an angle tower, tall narrow windows, and a verandah on chamfered posts, that figured so confidently as a "Tuscan Villa" in Downing's "Landscape Gardening in America." There was the same difference between the rude lithograph of the earlier house and the fine steel engraving of its successor (with a "specimen" weeping beech on the lawn) as between the buildings themselves. Mr. Raycie had reason to think well of his architect.

He thought well of most things related to himself by ties of blood or interest. No one had ever been quite sure that he made Mrs. Raycie happy, but he was known to have the highest opinion of her. So it was with his daughters, Sarah Anne and Mary Adeline, fresher replicas of the lymphatic Mrs. Raycie; no one would have sworn that they were quite at ease with their genial parent, yet every one knew how loud he was in their praises. But the most remarkable object within the range of Mr. Raycie's self-approval was his son Lewis. And yet, as Jameson Ledgely, who was given to speaking his mind, had once observed, you wouldn't have supposed young Lewis was exactly the kind of craft Halston would have turned out if he'd had the designing of his son and heir.

Mr. Raycie was a monumental man. His extent in height, width and thickness was so nearly the same that whichever way he was turned one had an almost equally broad view of him; and every inch of that mighty circumference was so exquisitely cared for that to a farmer's eye he might have suggested a great agricultural estate of which not an acre is untilled. Even his baldness, which was in proportion to the rest, looked as if it received a special daily polish; and on a hot day his whole person was like some wonderful example of the costliest irrigation. There was so much of him, and he had so many planes, that it was fascinating to watch each runnel of moisture follow its own particular watershed. Even on his large fresh-looking hands the drops divided, trickling in different ways from the ridges of the fingers; and as for his forehead and temples, and the raised cushion of cheek beneath each of his lower lids, every one of these slopes had its own particular stream, its hollow pools and sudden cataracts; and the sight was never unpleasant, because his whole vast bubbling surface was of such a clean and hearty pink, and the exuding moisture so perceptibly flavoured with expensive eau de Cologne and the best French soap.

Mrs. Raycie, though built on a less heroic scale, had a pale amplitude which, when she put on her best watered silk (the kind that stood alone), and framed her countenance in the innumerable blonde lace ruffles and clustered purple grapes of her newest Paris cap, almost balanced her husband's bulk. Yet from this full-rigged pair, as the Commodore would have put it, had issued the lean little runt of a Lewis, a shrimp of a baby, a shaver of a boy, and now a youth as scant as an ordinary man's midday shadow.

All these things, Lewis himself mused, dangling his legs from the verandah rail, were undoubtedly passing through the minds of the four gentlemen grouped about his father's bowl of cup.

Mr. Robert Huzzard, the banker, a tall broad man, who looked big in any company but Mr. Raycie's, leaned back, lifted his glass, and bowed to Lewis.

"Here's to the Grand Tour!"

"Don't perch on that rail like a sparrow, my boy," Mr. Raycie said reprovingly; and Lewis dropped to his feet, and returned Mr. Huzzard's bow.

"I wasn't thinking," he stammered. It was his too frequent excuse.

Mr. Ambrose Huzzard, the banker's younger brother, Mr. Ledgely and Mr. Donaldson Kent, all raised their glasses and cheerily echoed: "The Grand Tour!"

Lewis bowed again, and put his lips to the glass he had forgotten. In reality, he had eyes only for Mr. Donaldson Kent, his father's cousin, a silent man with a lean hawk-like profile, who looked like a retired Revolutionary hero, and lived in daily fear of the most trifling risk or responsibility.

To this prudent and circumspect citizen had come, some years earlier, the unexpected and altogether inexcusable demand that he should look after the daughter of his only brother, Julius Kent. Julius had died in Italy—well, that was his own business, if he chose to live there. But to let his wife die before him, and to leave a minor daughter, and a will entrusting her to the guardianship of his esteemed elder brother, Donaldson Kent Esquire, of Kent's Point, Long Island, and Great Jones Street, New York—well, as Mr. Kent himself said, and as his wife said for him, there had never been anything, anything whatever, in Mr. Kent's attitude or behaviour, to justify the ungrateful Julius (whose debts he had more than once paid) in laying on him this final burden.

The girl came. She was fourteen, she was considered plain, she was small and black and skinny. Her name was Beatrice, which was bad enough, and made worse by the fact that it had been shortened by ignorant foreigners to Treeshy. But she was eager, serviceable and good-tempered, and as Mr. and Mrs. Kent's friends pointed out, her plainness made everything easy. There were two Kent boys growing up, Bill and Donald; and if this penniless cousin had been compounded of cream and roses—well, she would have taken more watching, and might have rewarded the kindness of her uncle and aunt by some act of wicked ingratitude. But this risk being obviated by her appearance, they could be goodnatured to her without afterthought, and to be good-natured was natural to them. So, as the years passed, she gradually became the guardian of her guardians; since it was equally natural to Mr. and Mrs. Kent to throw themselves in helpless reliance on every one whom they did not nervously fear or mistrust.

"Yes, he's off on Monday," Mr. Raycie said, nodding sharply at Lewis, who had set down his glass after one sip.

"Empty it, you shirk!" the nod commanded; and Lewis, throwing back his head, gulped down the draught, though it almost stuck in his lean throat. He had already had to take two glasses, and even this scant conviviality was too much for him, and likely to result in a mood of excited volubility, followed by a morose evening and a head the next morning. And he wanted to keep his mind clear that day, and to think steadily and lucidly of Treeshy Kent.

Of course he couldn't marry her—yet. He was twenty-one that very day, and still entirely dependent on his father. And he wasn't altogether sorry to be going first on this Grand Tour. It was what he had always dreamed of, pined for, from the moment when his infant eyes had first been drawn to the prints of European cities in the long upper passage that smelt of matting. And all that Treeshy had told him about Italy had confirmed and intensified the longing. Oh, to have been going there with her—with her as his guide, his Beatrice! (For she had given him a little Dante of her father's, with a steel-engraved frontispiece of Beatrice; and his sister Mary Adeline, who had been taught Italian by one of the romantic Milanese exiles, had helped her brother out with the grammar.)

The thought of going to Italy with Treeshy was only a dream; but later, as man and wife, they would return there, and by that time, perhaps, it was Lewis who would be her guide, and reveal to her the historic marvels of her birth-place, of which after all she knew so little, except in minor domestic ways that were quaint but unimportant.

The prospect swelled her suitor's bosom, and reconciled

him to the idea of their separation. After all, he secretly felt himself to be still a boy, and it was as a man that he would return: he meant to tell her that when they met the next day. When he came back his character would be formed, his knowledge of life (which he already thought considerable) would be complete; and then no one could keep them apart. He smiled in advance to think how little his father's shouting and booming would impress a man on his return from the Grand Tour. . . .

The gentlemen were telling anecdotes about their own early experiences in Europe. None of them—not even Mr. Raycie—had travelled as extensively as it was intended that Lewis should; but the two Huzzards had been twice to England on banking matters, and Commodore Ledgely, a bold man, to France and Belgium as well—not to speak of his early experiences in the Far East. All three had kept a vivid and amused recollection, slightly tinged with disapprobation, of what they had seen—"Oh, those French wenches," the Commodore chuckled through his white teeth—but poor Mr. Kent, who had gone abroad on his honeymoon, had been caught in Paris by the revolution of 1830, had had the fever in Florence, and had nearly been arrested as a spy in Vienna; and the only satisfactory episode in this disastrous, and never repeated, adventure, had been the fact of his having been mistaken for the Duke of Wellington (as he was trying to slip out of a Viennese hotel in his courier's blue surtout) by a crowd who had been—"Well, very gratifying in their enthusiasm," Mr. Kent admitted.

"How my poor brother Julius could have lived in Europe!

Well, look at the consequences—" he used to say, as if poor Treeshy's plainness gave an awful point to his moral.

"There's one thing in Paris, my boy, that you must be warned against: those gambling-hells in the Pally Royle," Mr. Kent insisted. "I never set foot in the places myself; but a glance at the outside was enough."

"I knew a feller that was fleeced of a fortune there," Mr. Henry Huzzard confirmed; while the Commodore, at his tenth glass, chuckled with moist eyes: "The trollops, oh, the trollops—"

"As for Vienna—" said Mr. Kent.

"Even in London," said Mr. Ambrose Huzzard, "a young man must be on his look-out against gamblers. Every form of swindling is practised, and the touts are always on the look-out for greenhorns; a term," he added apologetically, "which they apply to any traveller new to the country."

"In Paris," said Mr. Kent, "I was once within an ace of being challenged to fight a duel." He fetched a sigh of horror and relief, and glanced reassuredly down the Sound in the direction of his own peaceful roof-tree.

"Oh, a duel," laughed the Commodore. "A man can fight duels here. I fought a dozen when I was a young feller in New Erleens." The Commodore's mother had been a southern lady, and after his father's death had spent some years with her parents in Louisiana, so that her son's varied experiences had begun early. "'Bout women," he smiled confidentially, holding out his empty glass to Mr. Raycie.

"The ladies—!" exclaimed Mr. Kent in a voice of warning.

The gentlemen rose to their feet, the Commodore quite

as promptly and steadily as the others. The drawing-room window opened, and from it emerged Mrs. Raycie, in a ruffled sarsenet dress and Point de Paris cap, followed by her two daughters in starched organdy with pink spencers. Mr. Raycie looked with proud approval at his womenkind.

"Gentlemen," said Mrs. Raycie, in a perfectly even voice, "supper is on the table, and if you will do Mr. Raycie and myself the favour—"

"The favour, ma'am," said Mr. Ambrose Huzzard, "is on your side, in so amiably inviting us."

Mrs. Raycie curtsied, the gentlemen bowed, and Mr. Raycie said: "Your arm to Mrs. Raycie, Huzzard. This little farewell party is a family affair, and the other gentlemen must content themselves with my two daughters. Sarah Anne, Mary Adeline—"

The Commodore and Mr. John Huzzard advanced ceremoniously toward the two girls, and Mr. Kent, being a cousin, closed the procession between Mr. Raycie and Lewis.

Oh, that supper-table! The vision of it used sometimes to rise before Lewis Raycie's eyes in outlandish foreign places; for though not a large or fastidious eater when he was at home, he was afterward, in lands of chestnut-flour and garlic and queer bearded sea-things, to suffer many pangs of hunger at the thought of that opulent board. In the centre stood the Raycie *épergne* of pierced silver, holding aloft a bunch of June roses surrounded by dangling baskets of sugared almonds and striped peppermints; and grouped about this decorative "motif" were Lowestoft platters heavy with piles of raspberries, strawberries and the first Delaware peaches.

An outer flanking of heaped-up cookies, crullers, strawberry short-cake, piping hot corn-bread and deep golden butter in moist blocks still bedewed from the muslin swathings of the dairy, led the eye to the Virginia ham in front of Mr. Raycie, and the twin dishes of scrambled eggs on toast and broiled blue-fish over which his wife presided. Lewis could never afterward fit into this intricate pattern the "side-dishes" of devilled turkey-legs and creamed chicken hash, the sliced cucumbers and tomatoes, the heavy silver jugs of butter-coloured cream, the floating-island, "slips" and lemon jellies that were somehow interwoven with the solider elements of the design; but they were all there, either together or successively, and so were the towering piles of waffles reeling on their foundations, and the slender silver jugs of maple syrup perpetually escorting them about the table as black Dinah replenished the supply.

They ate—oh, how they all ate!—though the ladies were supposed only to nibble; but the good things on Lewis's plate remained untouched until, ever and again, an admonishing glance from Mr. Raycie, or an entreating one from Mary Adeline, made him insert a languid fork into the heap.

And all the while Mr. Raycie continued to hold forth.

"A young man, in my opinion, before setting up for himself, must see the world; form his taste; fortify his judgment. He must study the most famous monuments, examine the organization of foreign societies, and the habits and customs of those older civilizations whose yoke it has been our glory to cast off. Though he may see in them much to deplore and to reprove—" ("Some of the gals, though,"

Commodore Ledgely was heard to interject)—"much that will make him give thanks for the privilege of having been born and brought up under our own Free Institutions, yet I believe he will also"—Mr. Raycie conceded it with magnanimity—"be able to learn much."

"The Sundays, though," Mr. Kent hazarded warningly; and Mrs. Raycie breathed across to her son: "Ah, that's what *I* say!"

Mr. Raycie did not like interruption; and he met it by growing visibly larger. His huge bulk hung a moment, like an avalanche, above the silence which followed Mr. Kent's interjection and Mrs. Raycie's murmur; then he crashed down on both.

"The Sundays—the Sundays? Well, what of the Sundays? What is there to frighten a good Episcopalian in what we call the Continental Sunday? I presume that we're all Churchmen here, eh? No puling Methodists or atheistical Unitarians at my table tonight, that I'm aware of? Nor will I offend the ladies of my household by assuming that they have secretly lent an ear to the Baptist ranter in the chapel at the foot of our lane. No? I thought not! Well, then, I say, what's all this flutter about the Papists? Far be it from me to approve of their heathenish doctrines—but, damn it, they go to church, don't they? And they have a real service, as we do, don't they? And real clergy, and not a lot of nondescripts dressed like laymen, and damned badly at that, who chat familiarly with the Almighty in their own vulgar lingo? No, sir"—he swung about on the shrinking Mr. Kent—"it's not the Church I'm afraid of in foreign countries, it's the sewers, sir!"

Mrs. Raycie had grown very pale: Lewis knew that she too was deeply perturbed about the sewers. "And the night-air," she scarce-audibly sighed.

But Mr. Raycie had taken up his main theme again. "In my opinion, if a young man travels at all, he must travel as extensively as his—er—means permit; must see as much of the world as he can. Those are my son's sailing orders, Commodore; and here's to his carrying them out to the best of his powers!"

Black Dinah, removing the Virginia ham, or rather such of its bony structure as alone remained on the dish, had managed to make room for a bowl of punch from which Mr. Raycie poured deep ladlefuls of perfumed fire into the glasses ranged before him on a silver tray. The gentlemen rose, the ladies smiled and wept, and Lewis's health and the success of the Grand Tour were toasted with an eloquence which caused Mrs. Raycie, with a hasty nod to her daughters, and a covering rustle of starched flounces, to shepherd them softly from the room.

"After all," Lewis heard her murmur to them on the threshold, "your father's using such language shows that he's in the best of humour with dear Lewis."

II

In spite of his enforced potations, Lewis Raycie was up the next morning before sunrise.

Unlatching his shutters without noise, he looked forth over the wet lawn merged in a blur of shrubberies, and the waters of the Sound dimly seen beneath a sky full of stars. His head ached but his heart glowed; what was before him was thrilling enough to clear a heavier brain than his.

He dressed quickly and completely (save for his shoes), and then, stripping the flowered quilt from his high mahogany bed, rolled it in a tight bundle under his arm. Thus enigmatically equipped he was feeling his way, shoes in hand, through the darkness of the upper story to the slippery oak stairs, when he was startled by a candle-gleam in the pitch-blackness of the hall below. He held his breath, and leaning over the stair-rail saw with amazement his sister Mary Adeline come forth, cloaked and bonneted, but also in stocking-feet, from the passage leading to the pantry. She too carried a double burden: her shoes and the candle in one hand, in the other a large covered basket that weighed down her bare arm.

Brother and sister stopped and stared at each other in the blue dusk: the upward slant of the candle-light distorted Mary Adeline's mild features, twisting them into a frightened grin as Lewis stole down to join her.

"Oh—" she whispered. "What in the world are you doing here? I was just getting together a few things for that poor young Mrs. Poe down the lane, who's so ill—before mother goes to the storeroom. You won't tell, will you?"

Lewis signalled his complicity, and cautiously slid open the bolt of the front door. They durst not say more till they were out of ear-shot. On the doorstep they sat down to put on their shoes; then they hastened on without a word through the ghostly shrubberies till they reached the gate into the lane.

"But you, Lewis?" the sister suddenly questioned, with an astonished stare at the rolled-up quilt under her brother's arm.

"Oh, I—. Look here, Addy—" he broke off and began to grope in his pocket—"I haven't much about me . . . the old gentleman keeps me as close as ever . . . but here's a dollar, if you think that poor Mrs. Poe could use it . . . I'd be too happy . . . consider it a privilege. . . ."

"Oh, Lewis, Lewis, how noble, how generous of you! Of course I can buy a few extra things with it . . . they never see meat unless I can bring them a bit, you know . . . and I fear she's dying of a decline . . . and she and her mother are so fiery-proud. . . ." She wept with gratitude, and Lewis drew a breath of relief. He had diverted her attention from the bed-quilt.

"Ah, there's the breeze," he murmured, sniffing the suddenly chilled air.

"Yes; I must be off; I must be back before the sun is up," said Mary Adeline anxiously, "and it would never do if mother knew—"

"She doesn't know of your visits to Mrs. Poe?"

A look of childish guile sharpened Mary Adeline's undeveloped face. "She *does*, of course; but yet she doesn't . . . we've arranged it so. You see, Mr. Poe's an Atheist; and so father—"

"I see," Lewis nodded. "Well, we part here; I'm off for

a swim," he said glibly. But abruptly he turned back and caught his sister's arm. "Sister, tell Mrs. Poe, please, that I heard her husband give a reading from his poems in New York two nights ago—"

("Oh, Lewis—*you*? But father says he's a blasphemer!")

"—And that he's a great poet—a Great Poet. Tell her that from me, will you, please, Mary Adeline?"

"Oh, brother, I couldn't . . . we never speak of him," the startled girl faltered, hurrying away.

In the cove where the Commodore's sloop had ridden a few hours earlier a biggish rowing-boat took the waking ripples. Young Raycie paddled out to her, fastened his skiff to the moorings, and hastily clambered into the boat.

From various recesses of his pockets he produced rope, string, a carpet-layer's needle, and other unexpected and incongruous tackle; then, lashing one of the oars across the top of the other, and jamming the latter upright between the forward thwart and the bow, he rigged the flowered bed-quilt on this mast, knotted a rope to the free end of the quilt, and sat down in the stern, one hand on the rudder, the other on his improvised sheet.

Venus, brooding silverly above a line of pale green sky, made a pool of glory in the sea as the dawn-breeze plumped the lover's sail. . . .

On the shelving pebbles of another cove, two or three miles down the Sound, Lewis Raycie lowered his queer sail and beached his boat. A clump of willows on the shingle-edge mysteriously stirred and parted, and Treeshy Kent was in his arms.

The sun was just pushing above a belt of low clouds in the east, spattering them with liquid gold, and Venus blanched as the light spread upward. But under the willows it was still dusk, a watery green dusk in which the secret murmurs of the night were caught.

"Treeshy—Treeshy!" the young man cried, kneeling beside her—and then, a moment later: "My angel, are you sure that no one guesses—?"

The girl gave a faint laugh which screwed up her funny nose. She leaned her head on his shoulder, her round forehead and rough braids pressed against his cheek, her hands in his, breathing quickly and joyfully.

"I thought I should never get here," Lewis grumbled, "with that ridiculous bed-quilt—and it'll be broad day soon! To think that I was of age yesterday, and must come to you in a boat rigged like a child's toy on a duck-pond! If you knew how it humiliates me—"

"What does it matter, dear, since you're of age now, and your own master?"

"But am I, though? He says so—but it's only on his own terms; only while I do what he wants! You'll see . . . I've a credit of ten thousand dollars . . . ten . . . thou . . . sand . . . d'you hear? . . . placed to my name in a London bank; and not a penny here to bless myself with meanwhile. . . . Why, Treeshy darling, why, what's the matter?"

She flung her arms about his neck, and through their innocent kisses he could taste her tears. "What *is* it, Treeshy?" he implored her.

"I . . . oh, I'd forgotten it was to be our last day together till you spoke of London—cruel, cruel!" she reproached him; and through the green twilight of the willows her eyes blazed on him like two stormy stars. No other eyes he knew could express such elemental rage as Treeshy's.

"You little spitfire, you!" he laughed back somewhat chokingly. "Yes, it's our last day—but not for long; at our age two years are not so very long, after all, are they? And when I come back to you I'll come as my own master, independent, free—come to claim you in face of everything and everybody! Think of that, darling, and be brave for my sake . . . brave and patient . . . as I mean to be!" he declared heroically.

"Oh, but you—you'll see other girls; heaps and heaps of them; in those wicked old countries where they're so lovely. My uncle Kent says the European countries are all wicked, even my own poor Italy. . . ."

"But *you*, Treeshy; you'll be seeing cousins Bill and Donald meanwhile—seeing them all day long and every day. And you know you've a weakness for that great hulk of a Bill. Ah, if only I stood six-foot-one in my stockings I'd go with an easier heart, you fickle child!" he tried to banter her.

"Fickle? Fickle? *Me*—oh, Lewis!"

He felt the premonitory sweep of sobs, and his untried courage failed him. It was delicious, in theory, to hold weeping beauty to one's breast, but terribly alarming, he found, in practice. There came a responsive twitching in his throat.

"No, no; firm as adamant, true as steel; that's what we both mean to be, isn't it, *cara*?"

"*Caro*, yes," she sighed, appeased.

"And you'll write to me regularly, Treeshy—long long letters? I may count on that, mayn't I, wherever I am? And they must all be numbered, every one of them, so that I shall know at once if I've missed one; remember!"

"And, Lewis, you'll wear them here?" (She touched his breast.) "Oh, not *all*," she added, laughing, "for they'd make such a big bundle that you'd soon have a hump in front like Pulcinella—but always at least the last one, just the last one. Promise!"

"Always, I promise—as long as they're kind," he said, still struggling to take a spirited line.

"Oh, Lewis, they will be, as long as yours are—and long long afterward. . . ."

Venus failed and vanished in the sun's uprising.

III

The crucial moment, Lewis had always known, would be not that of his farewell to Treeshy, but of his final interview with his father.

On that everything hung: his immediate future as well as his more distant prospects. As he stole home in the early sunlight, over the dew-drenched grass, he glanced up apprehensively at Mr. Raycie's windows, and thanked his stars that they were still tightly shuttered.

There was no doubt, as Mrs. Raycie said, that her husband's "using language" before ladies showed him to be in high good humour, relaxed and slippered, as it were—a state his family so seldom saw him in that Lewis had sometimes impertinently wondered to what awful descent from the clouds he and his two sisters owed their timorous being.

It was all very well to tell himself, as he often did, that the bulk of the money was his mother's, and that he could turn her round his little finger. What difference did that make? Mr. Raycie, the day after his marriage, had quietly taken over the management of his wife's property, and deducted, from the very moderate allowance he accorded her, all her little personal expenses, even to the postage-stamps she used, and the dollar she put in the plate every Sunday. He called the allowance her "pin-money," since, as he often reminded her, he paid all the household bills himself, so that Mrs. Raycie's quarterly pittance could be entirely devoted, if she chose, to frills and feathers.

"And will be, if you respect my wishes, my dear," he always added. "I like to see a handsome figure well set-off, and not to have our friends imagine, when they come to dine, that Mrs. Raycie is sick above-stairs, and I've replaced her by a poor relation in *allapacca*." In compliance with which Mrs. Raycie, at once flattered and terrified, spent her last penny in adorning herself and her daughters, and had to stint their bedroom fires, and the servants' meals, in order to find a penny for any private necessity.

Mr. Raycie had long since convinced his wife that this method of dealing with her, if not lavish, was suitable, and in fact "handsome"; when she spoke of the subject to her relations it was with tears of gratitude for her husband's kindness in assuming the management of her property. As he managed it exceedingly well, her hard-headed brothers (glad to have the responsibility off their hands, and convinced that, if left to herself, she would have muddled her money away in ill-advised charities) were disposed to share her approval of Mr. Raycie; though her old mother sometimes said helplessly: "When I think that Lucy Ann can't as much as have a drop of gruel brought up to her without his weighing the oatmeal. . . ." But even that was only whispered, lest Mr. Raycie's mysterious faculty of hearing what was said behind his back should bring sudden reprisals on the venerable lady to whom he always alluded, with a tremor in his genial voice, as "my dear mother-in-law—unless indeed she will allow me to call her, more briefly but more truly, my dear mother."

To Lewis, hitherto, Mr. Raycie had meted the same measure as to the females of the household. He had dressed him well, educated him expensively, lauded him to the skies—and counted every penny of his allowance. Yet there was a difference; and Lewis was as well aware of it as any one.

The dream, the ambition, the passion of Mr. Raycie's life, was (as his son knew) to found a Family; and he had only Lewis to found it with. He believed in primogeniture, in heirlooms, in entailed estates, in all the ritual of the English "landed" tradition. No one was louder than he in praise of the democratic institutions under which he lived; but he never thought of them as affecting that more private but more important institution, the Family; and to the Family all his care and all his thoughts were given. The result, as Lewis dimly guessed, was, that upon his own shrinking and inadequate head was centred all the passion contained in the vast expanse of Mr. Raycie's breast. Lewis was his very own, and Lewis represented what was most dear to him; and for both these reasons Mr. Raycie set an inordinate value on the boy (a quite different thing, Lewis thought from loving him).

Mr. Raycie was particularly proud of his son's taste for letters. Himself not a wholly unread man, he admired intensely what he called the "cultivated gentleman"—and that was what Lewis was evidently going to be. Could he have combined with this tendency a manlier frame, and an interest in the few forms of sport then popular among gentlemen, Mr. Raycie's satisfaction would have been complete; but whose is, in this disappointing world? Meanwhile he flattered himself that, Lewis being still young and malleable, and his health certainly mending, two years of travel and adventure might send him back a very different figure, physically as well as mentally. Mr. Raycie had himself travelled in his youth, and was persuaded that the experience was formative; he secretly hoped for the return of a bronzed and broadened Lewis, seasoned by independence and adventure, and having discreetly sown his wild oats in foreign pastures, where they would not contaminate the home crop.

All this Lewis guessed; and he guessed as well that these two wander-years were intended by Mr. Raycie to lead up to a marriage and an establishment after Mr. Raycie's own heart, but in which Lewis's was not to have even a consulting voice.

"He's going to give me all the advantages—for his own purpose," the young man summed it up as he went down to join the family at the breakfast table.

Mr. Raycie was never more resplendent than at that moment of the day and season. His spotless white duck trousers, strapped under kid boots, his thin kerseymere coat, and drab *piqué* waistcoat crossed below a snowy stock, made him look as fresh as the morning and as appetizing as the peaches and cream banked before him.

Opposite sat Mrs. Raycie, immaculate also, but paler than usual, as became a mother about to part from her only son; and between the two was Sarah Anne, unusually pink, and apparently occupied in trying to screen her sister's empty seat. Lewis greeted them, and seated himself at his mother's right.

Mr. Raycie drew out his *guillochée* repeating watch, and detaching it from its heavy gold chain laid it on the table beside him.

"Mary Adeline is late again. It is a somewhat unusual thing for a sister to be late at the last meal she is to take—for two years—with her only brother."

"Oh, Mr. Raycie!" Mrs. Raycie faltered.

"I say, the idea is peculiar. Perhaps," said Mr. Raycie sarcastically, "I am going to be blessed with a *peculiar* daughter."

"I'm afraid Mary Adeline is beginning a sick headache, sir. She tried to get up, but really could not," said Sarah Anne in a rush.

Mr. Raycie's only reply was to arch ironic eyebrows, and Lewis hastily intervened: "I'm sorry, sir; but it may be my fault—"

Mrs. Raycie paled, Sarah Anne, purpled, and Mr. Raycie echoed with punctilious incredulity: "Your—fault?"

"In being the occasion, sir, of last night's too-sumptuous festivity—"

"Ha—ha—ha!" Mr. Raycie laughed, his thunders instantly dispelled.

He pushed back his chair and nodded to his son with a smile; and the two, leaving the ladies to wash up the teacups (as was still the habit in genteel families) betook themselves to Mr. Raycie's study.

What Mr. Raycie studied in this apartment—except the accounts, and ways of making himself unpleasant to his family—Lewis had never been able to discover. It was a small bare formidable room; and the young man, who never crossed the threshold but with a sinking of his heart, felt it sink lower than ever. "*Now*!" he thought.

Mr. Raycie took the only easy-chair, and began.

"My dear fellow, our time is short, but long enough for what I have to say. In a few hours you will be setting out on your great journey: an important event in the life of any young man. Your talents and character—combined with your means of improving the opportunity—make me hope that in your case it will be decisive. I expect you to come home from this trip a man—"

So far, it was all to order, so to speak; Lewis could have recited it beforehand. He bent his head in acquiescence.

"A man," Mr. Raycie repeated, "prepared to play a part, a considerable part, in the social life of the community. I expect you to be a figure in New York; and I shall give you the means to be so." He cleared his throat. "But means are not enough—though you must never forget that they are essential. Education, polish, experience of the world; these are what so many of our men of standing lack. What do they know of Art or Letters? We have had little time here to produce either as yet—you spoke?" Mr. Raycie broke off with a crushing courtesy.

"I—oh, no," his son stammered.

"Ah; I thought you might be about to allude to certain blasphemous penny-a-liners whose poetic ravings are said to have given them a kind of pothouse notoriety."

Lewis reddened at the allusion but was silent, and his father went on:

"Where is our Byron—our Scott—our Shakespeare? And in painting it is the same. Where are our Old Masters? We are not without contemporary talent; but for works of genius we must still look to the past; we must, in most cases, content ourselves with copies. . . . Ah, here, I know, my dear boy, I touch a responsive chord! Your love of the arts has not passed unperceived; and I mean, I desire, to do all I can to encourage it. Your future position in the world—your duties and obligations as a gentleman and a man of fortune—will not permit you to become, yourself, an eminent painter or a famous sculptor; but I shall raise no objection to your dabbling in these arts as an amateur—at least while you are travelling abroad. It will form your taste, strengthen your judgment, and give you, I hope, the discernment necessary to select for me a few masterpieces which shall *not* be copies. Copies," Mr. Raycie pursued with a deepening emphasis, "are for the less discriminating, or for those less blessed with this world's goods. Yes, my dear Lewis, I wish to create a gallery: a gallery of Heirlooms. Your mother participates in this ambition—she desires to see on our walls a few original specimens of the Italian genius. Raphael, I fear, we can hardly aspire to; but a Domenichino, an Albano, a Carlo Dolci, a Guercino, a Carlo Maratta—one or two of Salvator Rosa's noble landscapes . . . you see my idea? There shall be a Raycie Gallery; and it shall be your mission to get together its nucleus." Mr. Raycie paused, and mopped his flowing forehead. "I believe I could have given my son no task more to his liking."

"Oh, no, sir, none indeed!" Lewis cried, flushing and paling. He had in fact never suspected this part of his father's plan, and his heart swelled with the honour of so unforeseen a mission. Nothing, in truth, could have made him prouder or happier. For a moment he forgot love, forgot Treeshy, forgot everything but the rapture of moving among the masterpieces of which he had so long dreamed, moving not as a mere hungry spectator but as one whose privilege it should at least be to single out and carry away some of the lesser treasures. He could hardly take in what had happened, and the shock of the announcement left him, as usual, inarticulate.

He heard his father booming on, developing the plan,

explaining with his usual pompous precision that one of the partners of the London bank in which Lewis's funds were deposited was himself a noted collector, and had agreed to provide the young traveller with letters of introduction to other connoisseurs, both in France and Italy, so that Lewis's acquisitions might be made under the most enlightened guidance.

"It is," Mr. Raycie concluded, "in order to put you on a footing of equality with the best collectors that I have placed such a large sum at your disposal. I reckon that for ten thousand dollars you can travel for two years in the very best style; and I mean to place another five thousand to your credit"—he paused, and let the syllables drop slowly into his son's brain: "five thousand dollars for the purchase of works of art, which eventually—remember—will be yours; and will be handed on, I trust, to your sons' sons as long as the name of Raycie survives"—a length of time, Mr. Raycie's tone seemed to imply, hardly to be measured in periods less extensive than those of the Egyptian dynasties.

Lewis heard him with a whirling brain. *Five thousand dollars!* The sum seemed so enormous, even in dollars, and so incalculably larger when translated into any continental currency, that he wondered why his father, in advance, had given up all hope of a Raphael. . . . "If I travel economically," he said to himself, "and deny myself unnecessary luxuries, I may yet be able to surprise him by bringing one back. And my mother—how magnanimous, how splendid! Now I see why she has consented to all the little economies that sometimes seemed so paltry and so humiliating. . . ."

The young man's eyes filled with tears, but he was still silent, though he longed as never before to express his gratitude and admiration to his father. He had entered the study expecting a parting sermon on the subject of thrift, coupled with the prospective announcement of a "suitable establishment" (he could even guess the particular Huzzard girl his father had in view); and instead he had been told to spend his princely allowance in a princely manner, and to return home with a gallery of masterpieces. "At least," he murmured to himself, "it shall contain a Correggio."

"Well, sir?" Mr. Raycie boomed.

"Oh, sir—" his son cried, and flung himself on the vast slope of the parental waistcoat.

Amid all these accumulated joys there murmured deep down in him the thought that nothing had been said or done to interfere with his secret plans about Treeshy. It seemed almost as if his father had tacitly accepted the idea of their unmentioned engagement; and Lewis felt half guilty at not confessing to it then and there. But the gods are formidable even when they unbend; never more so, perhaps, than at such moments. . . .

PART II

IV

Lewis Raycie stood on a projecting rock and surveyed the sublime spectacle of Mont Blanc.

It was a brilliant August day, and the air, at that height, was already so sharp that he had had to put on his fur-lined pelisse. Behind him, at a respectful distance, was the travelling servant who, at a signal, had brought it up to him; below, in the bend of the mountain road, stood the light and elegant carriage which had carried him thus far on his travels.

Scarcely more than a year had passed since he had waved a farewell to New York from the deck of the packet-ship headed down the bay; yet, to the young man confidently facing Mont Blanc, nothing seemed left in him of that fluid and insubstantial being, the former Lewis Raycie, save a lurking and abeyant fear of Mr. Raycie senior. Even that, however, was so attenuated by distance and time, so far sunk below the horizon, and anchored on the far side of the globe, that it stirred in its sleep only when a handsomely folded and wafered letter in his parent's writing was handed out across the desk of some continental counting-house. Mr. Raycie senior did not write often, and when he did it was in a bland and stilted strain. He felt at a disadvantage on paper, and his natural sarcasm was swamped in the rolling periods which it cost him hours of labour to bring forth; so that the dreaded quality lurked for his son only in the curve of certain letters, and in a positively awful way of writing out, at full length, the word *Esquire*.

It was not that Lewis had broken with all the memories of his past of a year ago. Many still lingered in him, or rather had been transferred to the new man he had become—as for instance his tenderness for Treeshy Kent, which, somewhat to his surprise, had obstinately resisted all the assaults of English keepsake beauties and almond-eyed houris of the East. It startled him, at times, to find Treeshy's short dusky face, with its round forehead, the widely spaced eyes and the high cheek-bones, starting out at him suddenly in the street of some legendary town, or in a landscape of languid beauty, just as he had now and again been arrested in an exotic garden by the very scent of the verbena under the verandah at home. His travels had confirmed rather than weakened the family view of Treeshy's plainness; she could not be made to fit into any of the patterns of female beauty so far submitted to him; yet there she was, ensconced in his new heart and mind as deeply as in the old, though her kisses seemed less vivid, and the peculiar rough notes of her voice hardly reached him. Sometimes, half irritably, he said to himself that with an effort he could disperse her once for all; yet she lived on in him, unseen yet ineffaceable, like the image on a daguerreotype plate, no less there because so often invisible.

To the new Lewis, however, the whole business was less important than he had once thought it. His suddenly acquired maturity made Treeshy seem a petted child rather than the guide, the Beatrice, he had once considered her; and he promised himself, with an elderly smile, that as soon as he got to Italy he would write her the long letter for which he was now considerably in her debt.

His travels had first carried him to England. There he spent some weeks in collecting letters and recommendations for his tour, in purchasing his travelling-carriage and its numerous appurtenances, and in driving in it from cathedral town to storied castle, omitting nothing, from Abbotsford to Kenilworth, which deserved the attention of a cultivated mind. From England he crossed to Calais, moving slowly southward to the Mediterranean; and there, taking ship for the Piræus, he plunged into pure romance, and the tourist became a Giaour.

It was the East which had made him into a new Lewis Raycie; the East, so squalid and splendid, so pestilent and so poetic, so full of knavery and romance and fleas and nightingales, and so different, alike in its glories and its dirt, from what his studious youth had dreamed. After Smyrna and the bazaars, after Damascus and Palmyra, the Acropolis, Mytilene and Sunium, what could be left in his mind of Canal Street and the lawn above the Sound? Even the mosquitoes, which seemed at first the only connecting link, were different, because he fought with them in scenes so different; and a young gentleman who had journeyed across the desert in Arabian dress, slept under goats'-hair tents, been attacked by robbers in the Peloponnesus and despoiled by his own escort at Baalbek, and by customs' officials everywhere, could not but look with a smile on the terrors that walk New York and the Hudson river. Encased in security and monotony, that other Lewis Raycie, when his little figure bobbed up to the surface, seemed like a new-born babe preserved in alcohol. Even Mr. Raycie senior's thunders were now no more than the far-off murmur of summer lightning on a perfect evening. Had Mr. Raycie ever really frightened Lewis? Why, now he was not even frightened by Mont Blanc!

He was still gazing with a sense of easy equality at its awful pinnacles when another travelling-carriage paused near his own, and a young man, eagerly jumping from it, and also followed by a servant with a cloak, began to mount the slope. Lewis at once recognized the carriage, and the light springing figure of the young man, his blue coat and swelling stock, and the scar slightly distorting his handsome and eloquent mouth. It was the Englishman who had arrived at the Montanvert inn the night before with a valet, a guide, and such a cargo of books, maps and sketching-materials as threatened to overshadow even Lewis's outfit.

Lewis, at first, had not been greatly drawn to the newcomer, who, seated aloof in the dining-room, seemed not to see his fellow-traveller. The truth was that Lewis was dying for a little conversation. His astonishing experiences were so tightly packed in him (with no outlet save the meagre trickle of his nightly diary) that he felt they would soon melt into the vague blur of other people's travels unless he could give them fresh reality by talking them over. And the stranger with the deep-blue eyes that matched his coat, the scarred cheek and eloquent lip, seemed to Lewis a worthy listener. The Englishman appeared to think otherwise. He preserved an air of moody abstraction, which Lewis's vanity imagined him to have put on as the gods becloud themselves for their secret errands; and the curtness of his good-night was (Lewis flattered himself) surpassed only by the young New Yorker's.

But today all was different. The stranger advanced affably, raised his hat from his tossed statue-like hair, and enquired with a smile: "Are you by any chance interested in the forms of cirrous clouds?"

His voice was as sweet as his smile, and the two were reinforced by a glance so winning that it made the odd question seem not only pertinent but natural. Lewis, though surprised, was not disconcerted. He merely coloured with the unwonted sense of his ignorance, and replied ingenuously: "I believe, sir, I am interested in everything."

"A noble answer!" cried the other, and held out his hand.

"But I must add," Lewis continued with courageous honesty, "that I have never as yet had occasion to occupy myself particularly with the forms of cirrous clouds."

His companion looked at him merrily. "That," said he, "is no reason why you shouldn't begin to do so now!" To which Lewis as merrily agreed. "For in order to be interested in things," the other continued more gravely, "it is only necessary to see them; and I believe I am not wrong in saying that you are one of the privileged beings to whom the seeing eye has been given."

Lewis blushed his agreement, and his interlocutor continued: "You are one of those who have been on the road to Damascus."

"On the road? I've been to the place itself!" the wanderer exclaimed, bursting with the particulars of his travels; and then blushed more deeply at the perception that the other's use of the name had of course been figurative.

The young Englishman's face lit up. "You've been to Damascus—literally been there yourself? But that may be almost as interesting, in its quite different way, as the formation of clouds or lichens. For the present," he continued with a gesture toward the mountain, "I must devote myself to the extremely inadequate rendering of some of these delicate *aiguilles*; a bit of drudgery not likely to interest you in the face of so sublime a scene. But perhaps this evening—if, as I think, we are staying in the same inn—you will give me a few minutes of your society, and tell me something of your travels. My father," he added with his engaging smile, "has had packed with my paint-brushes a few bottles of a wholly trustworthy Madeira; and if you will favour me with your company at dinner. . . ."

He signed to his servant to undo the sketching materials, spread his cloak on the rock, and was already lost in his task as Lewis descended to the carriage.

The Madeira proved as trustworthy as his host had promised. Perhaps it was its exceptional quality which threw such a golden lustre over the dinner; unless it were rather the conversation of the blue-eyed Englishman which made Lewis Raycie, always a small drinker, feel that in his company every drop was nectar.

When Lewis joined his host it had been with the secret hope of at last being able to talk; but when the evening was over (and they kept it up to the small hours) he perceived that he had chiefly listened. Yet there had been no sense of suppression, of thwarted volubility; he had been given all the openings he wanted. Only, whenever he produced a little fact it was instantly overflowed by the other's imagination till it burned like a dull pebble tossed into a rushing stream. For whatever Lewis said was seen by his companion from a new angle, and suggested a new train of thought; each commonplace item of experience became a many-faceted crystal flashing with unexpected fires. The young Englishman's mind moved in a world of associations and references far more richly peopled than Lewis's; but his eager communicativeness, his directness of speech and manner, instantly opened its gates to the simpler youth. It was certainly not the Madeira which sped the hours and flooded them with magic; but the magic gave the Madeira—excellent, and reputed of its kind, as Lewis afterward learned—a taste no other vintage was to have for him.

"Oh, but we must meet again in Italy—there are many things there that I could perhaps help you to see," the young Englishman declared as they swore eternal friendship on the stairs of the sleeping inn.

V

It was in a tiny Venetian church, no more than a chapel, that Lewis Raycie's eyes had been unsealed—in a dull-looking little church not even mentioned in the guide-books. But for his chance encounter with the young Englishman in the shadow of Mont Blanc, Lewis would never have heard of the place; but then what else that was worth knowing would he ever have heard of, he wondered?

He had stood a long time looking at the frescoes, put off at first—he could admit it now—by a certain stiffness in the attitudes of the people, by the childish elaboration of their dress (so different from the noble draperies which Sir Joshua's Discourses on Art had taught him to admire in the great painters), and by the innocent inexpressive look in their young faces—for even the gray-beards seemed young. And then suddenly his gaze had lit on one of these faces in particular: that of a girl with round cheeks, high cheek-bones and widely set eyes under an intricate head-dress of pearl-woven braids. Why, it was Treeshy—Treeshy Kent to the life! And so far from being thought "plain," the young lady was no other than the peerless princess about whom the tale revolved. And what a fairy-land she lived in—full of lithe youths and round-faced pouting maidens, rosy old men and burnished blackamoors, pretty birds and cats and nibbling rabbits—and all involved and enclosed in golden balustrades, in colonnades of pink and blue, laurel-garlands festooned from ivory balconies, and domes and minarets against summer seas! Lewis's imagination lost itself in the scene; he forgot to regret the noble draperies, the exalted sentiments, the fuliginous backgrounds, of the artists he had come to Italy to admire—forgot Sassoferrato, Guido Reni, Carlo Dolce, Lo Spagnoletto, the Carracci, and even the Transfiguration of Raphael, though he knew it to be the greatest picture in the world.

After that he had seen almost everything else that Italian art had to offer; had been to Florence, Naples, Rome; to Bologna to study the Eclectic School, to Parma to examine the Correggios and the Giulio Romanos. But that first vision had laid a magic seed between his lips; the seed that makes you hear what the birds say and the grasses whisper. Even if his English friend had not continued at his side, pointing out, explaining, inspiring, Lewis Raycie flattered himself that the round face of the little Saint Ursula would have led him safely and confidently past all her rivals. She had become his touchstone, his star: how insipid seemed to him all the sheep-faced Virgins draped in red and blue paint after he had looked into her wondering girlish eyes and traced the elaborate pattern of her brocades! He could remember now, quite distinctly, the day when he had given up even Beatrice Cenci . . . and as for that fat naked Magdalen of Carlo Dolce's, lolling over the book she was not reading, and ogling the spectator in the good old way . . . faugh! Saint Ursula did not need to rescue him from *her*. . . .

His eyes had been opened to a new world of art. And this world it was his mission to reveal to others—he, the insignificant and ignorant Lewis Raycie, as "but for the grace of

God," and that chance encounter on Mont Blanc, he might have gone on being to the end! He shuddered to think of the army of Neapolitan beggar-boys, bituminous monks, whirling prophets, languishing Madonnas and pink-rumped *amorini* who might have been travelling home with him in the hold of the fast new steam-packet.

His excitement had something of the apostle's ecstasy. He was not only, in a few hours, to embrace Treeshy, and be reunited to his honoured parents; he was also to go forth and preach the new gospel to them that sat in the darkness of Salvator Rosa and Lo Spagnoletto. . . .

The first thing that struck Lewis was the smallness of the house on the Sound, and the largeness of Mr. Raycie.

He had expected to receive the opposite impression. In his recollection the varnished Tuscan villa had retained something of its impressiveness, even when compared to its supposed originals. Perhaps the very contrast between their draughty distances and naked floors, and the expensive carpets and bright fires of High Point, magnified his memory of the latter—there were moments when the thought of its groaning board certainly added to the effect. But the image of Mr. Raycie had meanwhile dwindled. Everything about him, as his son looked back, seemed narrow, juvenile, almost childish. His bluster about Edgar Poe, for instance—true poet still to Lewis, though he had since heard richer notes; his fussy tyranny of his womenkind; his unconscious but total ignorance of most of the things, books, people, ideas, that now filled his son's mind; above all, the arrogance and incompetence of his artistic judgments. Beyond a narrow range of reading—mostly, Lewis suspected, culled in drowsy after-dinner snatches from Knight's "Half-hours with the Best Authors"—Mr. Raycie made no pretence to book-learning; left *that*, as he handsomely said, "to the professors." But on matters of art he was dogmatic and explicit, prepared to justify his opinions by the citing of eminent authorities and of market-prices, and quite clear, as his farewell talk with his son had shown, as to which Old Masters should be privileged to figure in the Raycie collection.

The young man felt no impatience of these judgments. America was a long way from Europe, and it was many years since Mr. Raycie had travelled. He could hardly be blamed for not knowing that the things he admired were no longer admirable, still less for not knowing why. The pictures before which Lewis had knelt in spirit had been virtually undiscovered, even by art-students and critics, in his father's youth. How was an American gentleman, filled with his own self-importance, and paying his courier the highest salary to show him the accredited "Masterpieces"—how was he to guess that whenever he stood rapt before a Sassoferrato or a Carlo Dolce one of those unknown treasures lurked near by under dust and cobwebs?

No; Lewis felt only tolerance and understanding. Such a view was not one to magnify the paternal image; but when the young man entered the study where Mr. Raycie sat immobilized by gout, the swathed leg stretched along his sofa seemed only another reason for indulgence. . . .

Perhaps, Lewis thought afterward, it was his father's

prone position, the way his great bulk billowed over the sofa, and the lame leg reached out like a mountain-ridge, that made him suddenly seem to fill the room; or else the sound of his voice booming irritably across the threshold, and scattering Mrs. Raycie and the girls with a fierce: "And now, ladies, if the hugging and kissing are over, I should be glad of a moment with my son." But it was odd that, after mother and daughters had withdrawn with all their hoops and flounces, the study seemed to grow even smaller, and Lewis himself to feel more like a David without the pebble.

"Well, my boy," his father cried, crimson and puffing, "here you are at home again, with many adventures to relate, no doubt; and a few masterpieces to show me, as I gather from the drafts on my exchequer."

"Oh, as to the masterpieces, sir, certainly," Lewis simpered, wondering why his voice sounded so fluty, and his smile was produced with such a conscious muscular effort.

"Good—good," Mr. Raycie approved, waving a violet hand which seemed to be ripening for a bandage. "Reedy carried out my orders, I presume? Saw to it that the paintings were deposited with the bulk of your luggage in Canal Street?"

"Oh, yes, sir; Mr. Reedy was on the dock with precise instructions. You know he always carries out your orders," Lewis ventured with a faint irony.

Mr. Raycie stared. "Mr. Reedy," he said, "does what I tell him, if that's what you mean; otherwise he would hardly have been in my employ for over thirty years."

Lewis was silent, and his father examined him critically. "You appear to have filled out; your health is satisfactory?

Well . . . well. . . . Mr. Robert Huzzard and his daughters are dining here this evening, by the way, and will no doubt be expecting to see the latest French novelties in stocks and waistcoats. Malvina has become a very elegant figure, your sisters tell me." Mr. Raycie chuckled, and Lewis thought: "I *knew* it was the oldest Huzzard girl!" while a slight chill ran down his spine.

"As to the pictures," Mr. Raycie pursued with growing animation, "I am laid low, as you see, by this cursèd affliction, and till the doctors get me up again, here must I lie and try to imagine how your treasures will look in the new gallery. And meanwhile, my dear boy, I need hardly say that no one is to be admitted to see them till they have been inspected by me and suitably hung. Reedy shall begin unpacking at once; and when we move to town next month Mrs. Raycie, God willing, shall give the handsomest evening party New York has yet seen, to show my son's collection, and perhaps . . . eh, well? . . . to celebrate another interesting event in his history."

Lewis met this with a faint but respectful gurgle, and before his blurred eyes rose the wistful face of Treeshy Kent.

"Ah, well, I shall see her tomorrow," he thought, taking heart again as soon as he was out of his father's presence.

VI

Mr. Raycie stood silent for a long time after making the round of the room in the Canal Street house where the unpacked pictures had been set out.

He had driven to town alone with Lewis, sternly rebuffing his daughters' timid hints, and Mrs. Raycie's mute but visible yearning to accompany him. Though the gout was over he was still weak and irritable, and Mrs. Raycie, fluttered at the thought of "crossing him," had swept the girls away at his first frown.

Lewis's hopes rose as he followed his parent's limping progress. The pictures, though standing on chairs and tables, and set clumsily askew to catch the light, bloomed out of the half-dusk of the empty house with a new and persuasive beauty. Ah, how right he had been—how inevitable that his father should own it!

Mr. Raycie halted in the middle of the room. He was still silent, and his face, so quick to frown and glare, wore the calm, almost expressionless look known to Lewis as the mask of inward perplexity. "Oh, of course it will take a little time," the son thought, tingling with the eagerness of youth.

At last, Mr. Raycie woke the echoes by clearing his throat; but the voice which issued from it was as inexpressive as his face. "It is singular," he said, "how little the best copies of the Old Masters resemble the originals. For these *are* Originals?" he questioned, suddenly swinging about on Lewis.

"Oh, absolutely, sir! Besides—" The young man was about to add: "No one would ever have taken the trouble to copy them"—but hastily checked himself.

"Besides——?"

"I meant, I had the most competent advice obtainable."

"So I assume; since it was the express condition on which I authorized your purchases."

Lewis felt himself shrinking and his father expanding; but he sent a glance along the wall, and beauty shed her reviving beam on him.

Mr. Raycie's brows projected ominously; but his face remained smooth and dubious. Once more he cast a slow glance about him.

"Let us," he said pleasantly, "begin with the Raphael." And it was evident that he did not know which way to turn.

"Oh, sir, a Raphael nowadays—I warned you it would be far beyond my budget."

Mr. Raycie's face fell slightly. "I had hoped nevertheless . . . for an inferior specimen. . . ." Then, with an effort: "The Sassoferrato, then."

Lewis felt more at his ease; he even ventured a respectful smile. "Sassoferrato is *all* inferior, isn't he? The fact is, he no longer stands . . . quite as he used to. . . ."

Mr. Raycie stood motionless: his eyes were vacuously fixed on the nearest picture.

"Sassoferrato . . . no longer . . . ?"

"Well, sir, *no*; not for a collection of this quality."

Lewis saw that he had at last struck the right note. Something large and uncomfortable appeared to struggle in Mr. Raycie's throat; then he gave a cough which might almost have been said to cast out Sassoferrato.

There was another pause before he pointed with his stick to a small picture representing a snub-nosed young woman with a high forehead and jewelled coif, against a background of delicately interwoven columbines. "Is *that*," he questioned, "your Carlo Dolce? The style is much the same, I see; but it seems to me lacking in his peculiar sentiment."

"Oh, but it's not a Carlo Dolce: it's a Piero della Francesca, sir!" burst in triumph from the trembling Lewis.

His father sternly faced him. "It's a *copy*, you mean? I thought so!"

"No, no; not a copy; it's by a great painter . . . a much greater. . . ."

Mr. Raycie had reddened sharply at his mistake. To conceal his natural annoyance he assumed a still more silken manner. "In that case," he said, "I think I should like to see the inferior painters first. Where *is* the Carlo Dolce?"

"There *is* no Carlo Dolce," said Lewis, white to the lips.

The young man's next distinct recollection was of standing, he knew not how long afterward, before the armchair in which his father had sunk down, almost as white and shaken as himself.

"This," stammered Mr. Raycie, "this is going to bring back my gout. . . ." But when Lewis entreated: "Oh, sir, do let us drive back quietly to the country, and give me a chance later to explain . . . to put my case" . . . the old gentleman had struck through the pleading with a furious wave of his stick.

"Explain later? Put your case later? It's just what I insist upon your doing here and now!" And Mr. Raycie added hoarsely, and as if in actual physical anguish: "I understand that young John Huzzard returned from Rome last week with a Raphael."

After that, Lewis heard himself—as if with the icy detachment of a spectator—marshalling his arguments, pleading the cause he hoped his pictures would have pleaded for him, dethroning the old Powers and Principalities, and setting up these new names in their place. It was first of all the names that stuck in Mr. Raycie's throat: after spending a life-time in committing to memory the correct pronunciation of words like Lo Spagnoletto and Giulio Romano, it was bad enough, his wrathful eyes seemed to say, to have to begin a new set of verbal gymnastics before you could be sure of saying to a friend with careless accuracy: "And *this* is my Giotto da Bondone."

But that was only the first shock, soon forgotten in the rush of greater tribulation. For one might conceivably learn how to pronounce Giotto da Bondone, and even enjoy doing so, provided the friend in question recognized the name and bowed to its authority. But to have your effort received by a blank stare, and the playful request: "You'll have to say that over again, please"—to know that, in going the round of the gallery (the Raycie Gallery!) the same stare and the same request were likely to be repeated before each picture; the bitterness of this was so great that Mr. Raycie, without exaggeration, might have likened his case to that of Agag.

"God! God! God! Carpatcher, you say this other fellow's called? Kept him back till the last because it's the gem of the collection, did you? Carpatcher—well, he'd have done better to stick to his trade. Something to do with those new European steam-cars, I suppose, eh?" Mr. Raycie was so incensed that his irony was less subtle than usual. "And Angelico you say did that kind of Noah's Ark soldier in pink armour on gold-leaf? Well, *there* I've caught you tripping, my boy. Not Angelico, Angelica; Angelica Kauffman was a lady. And the damned swindler who foisted that barbarous daub on you as a picture of hers deserves to be drawn and quartered—and shall be, sir, by God, if the law can reach him! He shall disgorge every penny he's rooked you out of, or my name's not Halston Raycie! A bargain . . . you say the thing was a *bargain*? Why, the price of a clean postage stamp would be too dear for it! God—my son; do you realize you had a *trust* to carry out?"

"Yes, sir, yes; and it's just because—"

"You might have written; you might at least have placed your views before me. . . ."

How could Lewis say: "If I had, I knew you'd have refused to let me buy the pictures?" He could only stammer: "I *did* allude to the revolution in taste . . . new names coming up . . . you may remember. . . ."

"Revolution! New names! Who says so? I had a letter last week from the London dealers to whom I especially recommended you, telling me that an undoubted Guido Reni was coming into the market this summer."

"Oh, the dealers—*they* don't know!"

"The dealers . . . don't? . . . Who does . . . except yourself?" Mr. Raycie pronounced in a white sneer.

Lewis, as white, still held his ground. "I wrote you, sir, about my friends; in Italy, and afterward in England."

"Well, God damn it, I never heard of one of *their* names

before, either; no more'n of these painters of yours here. I supplied you with the names of all the advisers you needed, and all the painters, too; I all but made the collection for you myself, before you started. . . . I was explicit enough, in all conscience, wasn't I?"

Lewis smiled faintly. "That's what I hoped the pictures would be. . . ."

"What? Be what? What'd you mean?"

"Be explicit. . . . Speak for themselves . . . make you see that their painters are already superseding some of the better-known. . . ."

Mr. Raycie gave an awful laugh. "They are, are they? In whose estimation? Your friends', I suppose. What's the name, again, of that fellow you met in Italy, who picked 'em out for you?"

"Ruskin—John Ruskin," said Lewis.

Mr. Raycie's laugh, prolonged, gathered up into itself a fresh shower of expletives. "Ruskin—Ruskin—just plain John Ruskin, eh? And who *is* this great John Ruskin, who sets God A'mighty right in his judgments? Who'd you say John Ruskin's father was, now?"

"A respected wine-merchant in London, sir."

Mr. Raycie ceased to laugh: he looked at his son with an expression of unutterable disgust.

"Retail?"

"I . . . believe so. . . ."

"Faugh!" said Mr. Raycie.

"It wasn't only Ruskin, father. . . . I told you of those other friends in London, whom I met on the way home. They inspected the pictures, and all of them agreed that . . . that the collection would some day be very valuable."

"*Some day*—did they give you a date . . . the month and the year? Ah, those other friends; yes. You said there was a Mr. Brown and a Mr. Hunt and a Mr. Rossiter, was it? Well, I never heard of any of those names, either—except perhaps in a trades' directory."

"It's not Rossiter, father: Dante Rossetti."

"Excuse me: Rossetti. And what does Mr. Dante Rossetti's father do? Sell macaroni, I presume?"

Lewis was silent, and Mr. Raycie went on, speaking now with a deadly steadiness: "The friends I sent you to were judges of art, sir; men who know what a picture's worth; not one of 'em but could pick out a genuine Raphael. Couldn't you find 'em when you got to England? Or hadn't they the time to spare for you? You'd better not," Mr. Raycie added, "tell me *that*, for I know how they'd have received your father's son."

"Oh, most kindly . . . they did indeed, sir. . . ."

"Ay; but that didn't suit you. You didn't *want* to be advised. You wanted to show off before a lot of ignoramuses like yourself. You wanted—how'd I know what you wanted? It's as if I'd never given you an instruction or laid a charge on you! And the money—God! Where'd it go to? Buying *this*? Nonsense—." Mr. Raycie raised himself heavily on his stick and fixed his angry eyes on his son. "Own up, Lewis; tell me they got it out of you at cards. Professional gamblers the lot, I make no doubt; your Ruskin and your Morris and your Rossiter. Make a business to pick up young American greenhorns on their travels, I daresay. . . . No? Not that, you say? Then—women? . . . God A'mighty, Lewis," gasped Mr. Raycie, tottering toward his son with outstretched stick, "I'm no blue-nosed Puritan, sir, and I'd a damn sight rather you told me you'd spent it on a woman, every penny of it, than let yourself be fleeced like a simpleton, buying these things that look more like cuts out o' Foxe's Book of Martyrs than Originals of the Old Masters for a Gentleman's Gallery. . . . Youth's youth. . . . Gad, sir, I've been young myself . . . a fellow's got to go through his apprenticeship. . . . Own up now: women?"

"Oh, not women——"

"Not even!" Mr. Raycie groaned. "All in pictures, then? Well, say no more to me now. . . . I'll get home, I'll get home. . . ." He cast a last apoplectic glance about the room. "The Raycie Gallery! That pack of bones and mummers' finery! . . . Why, let alone the rest, there's not a full-bodied female among 'em. . . . Do you know what those Madonnas of yours are like, my son? Why, there ain't one of 'em that don't remind me of a bad likeness of poor Treeshy Kent. . . . I should say you'd hired half the sign-painters of Europe to do her portrait for you—if I could imagine your wanting it. . . . No, sir! I don't need your arm," Mr. Raycie snarled, heaving his great bulk painfully across the hall. He withered Lewis with a last look from the doorstep. "And to buy *that* you overdrew your account?—No, I'll drive home alone."

VII

Mr. Raycie did not die till nearly a year later; but New York agreed it was the affair of the pictures that had killed him.

The day after his first and only sight of them he sent for his lawyer, and it became known that he had made a new will. Then he took to his bed with a return of the gout, and grew so rapidly worse that it was thought "only proper" to postpone the party Mrs. Raycie was to have given that autumn to inaugurate the gallery. This enabled the family to pass over in silence the question of the works of art themselves; but outside of the Raycie house, where they were never mentioned, they formed, that winter, a frequent and fruitful topic of discussion.

Only two persons besides Mr. Raycie were known to have seen them. One was Mr. Donaldson Kent, who owed the privilege to the fact of having once been to Italy; the other, Mr. Reedy, the agent, who had unpacked the pictures. Mr. Reedy, beset by Raycie cousins and old family friends, had replied with genuine humility: "Why, the truth is, I never was taught to see any difference between one picture and another, except as regards the size of them; and these struck me as smallish . . . on the small side, I would say. . . ."

Mr. Kent was known to have unbosomed himself to Mr. Raycie with considerable frankness—he went so far, it was rumoured, as to declare that he had never seen any pictures in Italy like those brought back by Lewis, and begged to doubt if they really came from there. But in public he maintained that noncommittal attitude which passed for prudence, but proceeded only from timidity; no one ever got anything from him but the guarded statement: "The subjects are wholly inoffensive."

It was believed that Mr. Raycie dared not consult the Huzzards. Young John Huzzard had just brought home a Raphael; it would have been hard not to avoid comparisons which would have been too galling. Neither to them, nor to any one else, did Mr. Raycie ever again allude to the Raycie Gallery. But when his will was opened it was found that he had bequeathed the pictures to his son. The rest of his property was left absolutely to his two daughters. The bulk of the estate was Mrs. Raycie's; but it was known that Mrs. Raycie had had her instructions, and among them, perhaps, was the order to fade away in her turn after six months of widowhood. When she had been laid beside her husband in Trinity church-yard her will (made in the same week as Mr. Raycie's, and obviously at his dictation) was found to allow five thousand dollars a year to Lewis during his lifetime; the residue of the fortune, which Mr. Raycie's thrift and good management had made into one of the largest in New York, was divided between the daughters. Of these, the one promptly married a Kent and the other a Huzzard; and the latter, Sarah Ann (who had never been Lewis's favourite), was wont to say in later years: "Oh, no, I never grudged my poor brother those funny old pictures. You see, we have a Raphael."

The house stood on the corner of Third Avenue and Tenth Street. It had lately come to Lewis Raycie as his share in the property of a distant cousin, who had made an "old New York will" under which all his kin benefited in proportion to their consanguinity. The neighbourhood was unfashionable, and the house in bad repair; but Mr. and Mrs. Lewis Raycie, who, since their marriage, had been living in retirement at Tarrytown, immediately moved into it.

Their arrival excited small attention. Within a year of his father's death, Lewis had married Treeshy Kent. The alliance had not been encouraged by Mr. and Mrs. Kent, who went so far as to say that their niece might have done better; but as that one of their sons who was still unmarried had always shown a lively sympathy for Treeshy, they yielded to the prudent thought that, after all, it was better than having her entangle Bill.

The Lewis Raycies had been four years married, and during that time had dropped out of the memory of New York as completely as if their exile had covered half a century. Neither of them had ever cut a great figure there. Treeshy had been nothing but the Kents' Cinderella, and Lewis's ephemeral importance, as heir to the Raycie millions, had been effaced by the painful episode which resulted in his being deprived of them.

So secluded was their way of living, and so much had it come to be a habit, that when Lewis announced that he had inherited Uncle Ebenezer's house his wife hardly looked up from the baby-blanket she was embroidering.

"Uncle Ebenezer's house in New York?"

He drew a deep breath. "Now I shall be able to show the pictures."

"Oh, Lewis—" She dropped the blanket. "Are we going to live there?"

"Certainly. But the house is so large that I shall turn the two corner rooms on the ground floor into a gallery. They are very suitably lighted. It was there that Cousin Ebenezer was laid out."

"Oh, Lewis——"

If anything could have made Lewis Raycie believe in his own strength of will it was his wife's attitude. Merely to hear that unquestioning murmur of submission was to feel something of his father's tyrannous strength arise in him; but with the wish to use it more humanely.

"You'll like that, Treeshy? It's been dull for you here, I know."

She flushed up. "Dull? With *you*, darling? Besides, I like the country. But I shall like Tenth Street too. Only—you said there were repairs?"

He nodded sternly. "I shall borrow money to make them. If necessary—" he lowered his voice—"I shall mortgage the pictures."

He saw her eyes fill. "Oh, but it won't be! There are so many ways still in which I can economize."

He laid his hand on hers and turned his profile toward her, because he knew it was so much stronger than his full face. He did not feel sure that she quite grasped his intention about the pictures; was not even certain that he wished her to. He went in to New York every week now, occupying himself mysteriously and importantly with plans, specifications and other business transactions with long names;

while Treeshy, through the hot summer months, sat in Tarrytown and waited for the baby.

A little girl was born at the end of the summer and christened Louisa; and when she was a few weeks old the Lewis Raycies left the country for New York.

"*Now*!" thought Lewis, as they bumped over the cobblestones of Tenth Street in the direction of Cousin Ebenezer's house.

The carriage stopped, he handed out his wife, the nurse followed with the baby, and they all stood and looked up at the house-front.

"Oh, Lewis—" Treeshy gasped; and even little Louisa set up a sympathetic wail.

Over the door—over Cousin Ebenezer's respectable, conservative and intensely private front-door—hung a large sign-board bearing, in gold letters on a black ground, the inscription:

GALLERY OF CHRISTIAN ART
OPEN ON WEEK-DAYS FROM 2 TO 4
ADMISSION 25 CENTS. CHILDREN 10 CENTS.

Lewis saw his wife turn pale, and pressed her arm in his. "Believe me, it's the only way to make the pictures known. And they *must* be made known," he said with a thrill of his old ardour.

"Yes, dear, of course. But . . . to every one? Publicly?"

"If we showed them only to our friends, of what use would it be? Their opinion is already formed."

She sighed her acknowledgment. "But the . . . the entrance fee. . . ."

"If we can afford it later, the gallery will be free. But meanwhile——"

"Oh, Lewis, I quite understand!" And clinging to him, the still-protesting baby in her wake, she passed with a dauntless step under the awful sign-board.

"At last I shall see the pictures properly lighted!" she exclaimed, and turned in the hall to fling her arms about her husband.

"It's all they need . . . to be appreciated," he answered, aglow with her encouragement.

Since his withdrawal from the world it had been a part of Lewis's system never to read the daily papers. His wife eagerly conformed to his example, and they lived in a little air-tight circle of aloofness, as if the cottage at Tarrytown had been situated in another and happier planet.

Lewis, nevertheless, the day after the opening of the Gallery of Christian Art, deemed it his duty to derogate from this attitude, and sallied forth secretly to buy the principal journals. When he re-entered his house he went straight up to the nursery where he knew that, at that hour, Treeshy would be giving the little girl her bath. But it was later than he supposed. The rite was over, the baby lay asleep in its modest cot, and the mother sat crouched by the fire, her face hidden in her hands. Lewis instantly guessed that she too had seen the papers.

"Treeshy—you mustn't . . . consider this of any consequence . . . ," he stammered.

She lifted a tear-stained face. "Oh, my darling! I thought you never read the papers."

"Not usually. But I thought it my duty——"

"Yes; I see. But, as you say, what earthly consequence——?"

"None whatever; we must just be patient and persist."

She hesitated, and then, her arms about him, her head on his breast: "Only, dearest, I've been counting up again, ever so carefully; and even if we give up fires everywhere but in the nursery, I'm afraid the wages of the door-keeper and the guardian . . . especially if the gallery's open to the public every day. . . ."

"I've thought of that already, too; and I myself shall hereafter act as door-keeper and guardian."

He kept his eyes on hers as he spoke. "This is the test," he thought. Her face paled under its brown glow, and the eyes dilated in her effort to check her tears. Then she said gaily: "That will be . . . very interesting, won't it, Lewis? Hearing what the people say. . . . Because, as they begin to know the pictures better, and to understand them, they can't fail to say very interesting things . . . can they?" She turned and caught up the sleeping Louisa. "Can they . . . oh, you darling—darling?"

Lewis turned away too. Not another woman in New

York would have been capable of that. He could hear all the town echoing with this new scandal of his showing the pictures himself—and she, so much more sensitive to ridicule, so much less carried away by apostolic ardour, how much louder must that mocking echo ring in her ears! But his pang was only momentary. The one thought that possessed him for any length of time was that of vindicating himself by making the pictures known; he could no longer fix his attention on lesser matters. The derision of illiterate journalists was not a thing to wince at; once let the pictures be seen by educated and intelligent people, and they would speak for themselves—especially if he were at hand to interpret them.

VIII

For a week or two a great many people came to the gallery; but, even with Lewis as interpreter, the pictures failed to make themselves heard. During the first days, indeed, owing to the unprecedented idea of holding a paying exhibition in a private house, and to the mockery of the newspapers, the Gallery of Christian Art was thronged with noisy curiosity-seekers; once the astonished metropolitan police had to be invited in to calm their comments and control their movements. But the name of "Christian Art" soon chilled this class of sightseer, and before long they were replaced by a dumb and respectable throng, who roamed vacantly through the rooms and out again, grumbling that it wasn't worth the money. Then these too diminished; and once the tide had turned, the ebb was rapid. Every day from two to four Lewis still sat shivering among his treasures, or patiently measured the length of the deserted gallery: as long as there was a chance of any one coming he would not admit that he was beaten. For the next visitor might always be the one who understood.

One snowy February day he had thus paced the rooms in unbroken solitude for above an hour when carriage-wheels stopped at the door. He hastened to open it, and in a great noise of silks his sister Sarah Anne Huzzard entered.

Lewis felt for a moment as he used to under his father's glance. Marriage and millions had given the moon-faced Sarah something of the Raycie awfulness; but her brother looked into her empty eyes, and his own kept their level.

"Well, Lewis," said Mrs. Huzzard with a simpering sternness, and caught her breath.

"Well, Sarah Anne—I'm happy that you've come to take a look at my pictures."

"I've come to see you and your wife." She gave another nervous gasp, shook out her flounces, and added in a rush: "And to ask you how much longer this . . . this spectacle is to continue. . . ."

"The exhibition?" Lewis smiled. She signed a flushed assent.

"Well, there has been a considerable falling-off lately in the number of visitors——"

"Thank heaven!" she interjected.

"But as long as I feel that any one wishes to come . . . I shall be here . . . to open the door, as you see."

She sent a shuddering glance about her. "Lewis—I wonder if you realize . . . ?"

"Oh, fully."

"Then *why* do you go on? Isn't it enough—aren't you satisfied?"

"With the effect they have produced?"

"With the effect *you* have produced—on your family and on the whole of New York. With the slur on poor Papa's memory."

"Papa left me the pictures, Sarah Anne."

"Yes. But not to make yourself a mountebank about them."

Lewis considered this impartially. "Are you sure? Perhaps, on the contrary, he did it for that very reason."

"Oh, don't heap more insults on our father's memory! Things are bad enough without that. How your wife can allow it I can't see. Do you ever consider the humiliation to *her*?"

Lewis gave another dry smile. "She's used to being humiliated. The Kents accustomed her to that."

Sarah Anne reddened. "I don't know why I should stay to be spoken to in this way. But I came with my husband's approval."

"Do you need that to come and see your brother?"

"I need it to—to make the offer I am about to make; and which he authorizes."

Lewis looked at her in surprise, and she purpled up to the lace ruffles inside her satin bonnet.

"Have you come to make an offer for my collection?" he asked her, humorously.

"You seem to take pleasure in insinuating preposterous things. But anything is better than this public slight on our name." Again she ran a shuddering glance over the pictures. "John and I," she announced, "are prepared to double the allowance mother left you on condition that this . . . this ends . . . for good. That that horrible sign is taken down tonight."

Lewis seemed mildly to weigh the proposal. "Thank you very much, Sarah Anne," he said at length. "I'm touched . . . touched and . . . and surprised . . . that you and John should have made this offer. But perhaps, before I decline it, you will accept *mine*: simply to show you my pictures. When once you've looked at them I think you'll understand——"

Mrs. Huzzard drew back hastily, her air of majesty collapsing. "Look at the pictures? Oh, thank you . . . but I can see them very well from here. And besides, I don't pretend to be a judge. . . ."

"Then come up and see Treeshy and the baby," said Lewis quietly.

She stared at him, embarrassed. "Oh, thank you," she stammered again; and as she prepared to follow him: "Then it's *no*, really no, Lewis? Do consider, my dear! You say yourself that hardly any one comes. What harm can there be in closing the place?"

"What—when tomorrow the man may come who understands?"

Mrs. Huzzard tossed her plumes despairingly and followed him in silence.

"What—Mary Adeline?" she exclaimed, pausing abruptly on the threshold of the nursery. Treeshy, as usual, sat holding her baby by the fire; and from a low seat opposite her rose a lady as richly furred and feathered as Mrs. Huzzard, but with far less assurance to carry off her furbelows. Mrs. Kent ran to Lewis and laid her plump cheek against his, while Treeshy greeted Sarah Anne.

"I had no idea you were here, Mary Adeline," Mrs. Huzzard murmured. It was clear that she had not imparted her philanthropic project to her sister, and was disturbed at the idea that Lewis might be about to do so. "I just dropped in for a minute," she continued, "to see that darling little pet of an angel child—" and she enveloped the astonished baby in her ample rustlings and flutterings.

"I'm very glad to see you here, Sarah Anne," Mary Adeline answered with simplicity.

"Ah, it's not for want of wishing that I haven't come before! Treeshy knows that, I hope. But the cares of a household like mine. . . ."

"Yes; and it's been so difficult to get about in the bad weather," Treeshy suggested sympathetically.

Mrs. Huzzard lifted the Raycie eyebrows. "Has it really? With two pairs of horses one hardly notices the weather. . . . Oh, the pretty, pretty, *pretty* baby! . . . Mary Adeline," Sarah Anne continued, turning severely to her sister, "I shall be happy to offer you a seat in my carriage if you're thinking of leaving."

But Mary Adeline was a married woman too. She raised her mild head and her glance crossed her sister's quietly. "My own carriage is at the door, thank you kindly, Sarah Anne," she said; and the baffled Sarah Anne withdrew on Lewis's arm. But a moment later the old habit of subordination reasserted itself. Mary Adeline's gentle countenance grew as timorous as a child's, and she gathered up her cloak in haste.

"Perhaps I was too quick. . . . I'm sure she meant it kindly," she exclaimed, overtaking Lewis as he turned to come up the stairs; and with a smile he stood watching his two sisters drive off together in the Huzzard coach.

He returned to the nursery, where Treeshy was still crooning over her daughter.

"Well, my dear," he said, "what do you suppose Sarah Anne came for?" And, in reply to her wondering gaze: "To buy me off from showing the pictures!"

His wife's indignation took just the form he could have wished. She simply went on with her rich cooing laugh and hugged the baby tighter. But Lewis felt the perverse desire to lay a still greater strain upon her loyalty.

"Offered to double my allowance, she and John, if only I'll take down the sign!"

"No one shall touch the sign!" Treeshy flamed.

"Not till I do," said her husband grimly.

She turned about and scanned him with anxious eyes. "Lewis . . . *you*?"

"Oh, my dear . . . they're right. . . . It can't go on forever. . . ." He went up to her, and put his arm about her and the child. "You've been braver than an army of heroes; but it won't do. The expenses have been a good deal heavier than I was led to expect. And I . . . I can't raise a mortgage on the pictures. Nobody will touch them."

She met this quickly. "No; I know. That was what Mary Adeline came about."

The blood rushed angrily to Lewis's temples. "Mary Adeline—how the devil did *she* hear of it?"

"Through Mr. Reedy, I suppose. But you must not be angry. She was kindness itself: she doesn't want you to close the gallery, Lewis . . . that is, not as long as you really continue to believe in it. . . . She and Donald Kent will lend us enough to go on with for a year longer. That is what she came to say."

For the first time since the struggle had begun, Lewis Raycie's throat was choked with tears. His faithful Mary Adeline! He had a sudden vision of her, stealing out of the house at High Point before daylight to carry a basket of scraps to the poor Mrs. Edgar Poe who was dying of a decline down the lane. . . . He laughed aloud in his joy.

"Dear old Mary Adeline! How magnificent of her! Enough to give me a whole year more. . . ." He pressed his wet cheek against his wife's in a long silence. "Well, dear," he said at length, "it's for you to say—do we accept?"

He held her off, questioningly, at arm's length, and her wan little smile met his own and mingled with it.

"Of course we accept!"

IX

Of the Raycie family, which prevailed so powerfully in the New York of the 'forties, only one of the name survived in my boyhood, half a century later. Like so many of the descendants of the proud little Colonial society, the Raycies had totally vanished, forgotten by everyone but a few old ladies, one or two genealogists and the sexton of Trinity Church, who kept the record of their graves.

The Raycie blood was of course still to be traced in various allied families: Kents, Huzzards, Cosbys and many others, proud to claim cousinship with a "Signer," but already indifferent or incurious as to the fate of his progeny. These old New Yorkers, who lived so well and spent their money so liberally, vanished like a pinch of dust when they disappeared from their pews and their dinner-tables.

If I happen to have been familiar with the name since my youth, it is chiefly because its one survivor was a distant cousin of my mother's, whom she sometimes took me to see on days when she thought I was likely to be good because I had been promised a treat for the morrow.

Old Miss Alethea Raycie lived in a house I had always heard spoken of as "Cousin Ebenezer's." It had evidently, in its day, been an admired specimen of domestic architecture; but was now regarded as the hideous though venerable relic of a bygone age. Miss Raycie, being crippled by rheumatism, sat above stairs in a large cold room, meagrely furnished with beadwork tables, rosewood étagères and portraits of pale sad-looking people in odd clothes. She herself was large and saturnine, with a battlemented black lace cap, and so deaf that she seemed a survival of forgotten days, a Rosetta Stone to which the clue was lost. Even to my mother, nursed in that vanished tradition, and knowing instinctively to whom Miss Raycie alluded when she spoke of Mary Adeline, Sarah Anne or Uncle Doctor, intercourse with her was difficult and languishing, and my juvenile interruptions were oftener encouraged than reproved.

In the course of one of these visits my eye, listlessly roaming, singled out among the pallid portraits a three-crayon drawing of a little girl with a large forehead and dark eyes, dressed in a plaid frock and embroidered pantalettes, and sitting on a grass-bank. I pulled my mother's sleeve to ask who she was, and my mother answered: "Ah, that was poor little Louisa Raycie, who died of a decline. How old was little Louisa when she died, Cousin Alethea?"

To batter this simple question into Cousin Alethea's brain was the affair of ten laborious minutes; and when the job was done, and Miss Raycie, with an air of mysterious displeasure, had dropped a deep "Eleven," my mother was too exhausted to continue. So she turned to me to add, with one of the private smiles we kept for each other: "It was the poor child who would have inherited the Raycie Gallery." But to a little boy of my age this item of information lacked interest, nor did I understand my mother's surreptitious amusement.

This far-off scene suddenly came back to me last year, when, on one of my infrequent visits to New York, I went to dine with my old friend, the banker, John Selwyn, and came to an astonished stand before the mantelpiece in his new library.

"Hal*lo*!" I said, looking up at the picture above the chimney.

My host squared his shoulders, thrust his hands into his pockets, and affected the air of modesty which people think it proper to assume when their possessions are admired. "The Macrino d'Alba? Y—yes . . . it was the only thing I managed to capture out of the Raycie collection."

"The only thing? Well——"

"Ah, but you should have seen the Mantegna; *and* the Giotto; *and* the Piero della Francesca—hang it, one of the most beautiful Piero della Francescas in the world. . . . A girl in profile, with her hair in a pearl net, against a background of columbines; *that* went back to Europe—the National Gallery, I believe. And the Carpaccio, the most exquisite little St. George . . . that went to California . . . *Lord*!" He sat down with the sigh of a hungry man turned away from a groaning board. "Well, it nearly broke me buying *this*!" he murmured, as if at least that fact were some consolation.

I was turning over my early memories in quest of a clue to what he spoke of as the Raycie collection, in a tone which implied that he was alluding to objects familiar to all art-lovers.

Suddenly: "They weren't poor little Louisa's pictures, by any chance?" I asked, remembering my mother's cryptic smile.

Selwyn looked at me perplexedly. "Who the deuce is poor little Louisa?" And, without waiting for my answer, he went on: "They were that fool Netta Cosby's until a year ago—and she never even knew it."

We looked at each other interrogatively, my friend perplexed at my ignorance, and I now absorbed in trying to run down the genealogy of Netta Cosby. I did so finally. "Netta Cosby—you don't mean Netta Kent, the one who married Jim Cosby?"

"That's it. They were cousins of the Raycies', and she inherited the pictures."

I continued to ponder. "I wanted awfully to marry her, the year I left Harvard," I said presently, more to myself than to my hearer.

"Well, if you had you'd have annexed a prize fool; *and* one of the most beautiful collections of Italian Primitives in the world."

"In the world?"

"Well—you wait till you see them; if you haven't already. And I seem to make out that you haven't—that you can't have. How long have you been in Japan? Four years? I thought so. Well, it was only last winter that Netta found out."

"Found out what?"

"What there was in old Alethea Raycie's attic. You must remember the old Miss Raycie who lived in that hideous house in Tenth Street when we were children. She was a cousin of your mother's, wasn't she? Well, the old fool lived there for nearly half a century, with five millions' worth of pictures shut up in the attic over her head. It seems they'd been there ever since the death of a poor young Raycie who collected them in Italy years and years ago. I don't know much about the story; I never was strong on genealogy, and the Raycies have always been rather dim to me. They were everybody's cousins, of course; but as far as one can make out that seems to have been their principal if not their only function. Oh—and I suppose the Raycie Building was called after them; only *they* didn't build it!

"But there was this one young fellow—I wish I could find out more about him. All that Netta seems to know (or to care, for that matter) is that when he was very young—barely out of college—he was sent to Italy by his father to buy Old Masters—in the 'forties, it must have been—and came back with this extraordinary, this unbelievable collection . . . a boy of that age! . . . and was disinherited by the old gentleman for bringing home such rubbish. The young fellow and his wife died ever so many years ago, both of them. It seems he was so laughed at for buying such pictures that they went away and lived like hermits in the depths of the country. There were some funny spectral portraits of them that old Alethea had up in her bedroom. Netta showed me one of them the last time I went to see her: a pathetic drawing of the only child, an anæmic little girl with a big forehead. Jove, but that must have been your little Louisa!"

I nodded. "In a plaid frock and embroidered pantalettes?"

"Yes, something of the sort. Well, when Louisa and her parents died, I suppose the pictures went to old Miss Raycie. At any rate, at some time or other—and it must have been longer ago than you or I can remember—the old lady inherited them with the Tenth Street house; and when *she* died, three or four years ago, her relations found she'd never even been upstairs to look at them."

"Well——?"

"Well, she died intestate, and Netta Kent—Netta Cosby—turned out to be the next of kin. There wasn't much to be got out of the estate (or so they thought) and, as the Cosbys are always hard up, the house in Tenth Street had to be sold, and the pictures were very nearly sent off to the auction room with all the rest of the stuff. But nobody supposed they would bring anything, and the auctioneer said that if you tried to sell pictures with carpets and bedding and kitchen furniture it always depreciated the whole thing; and so, as the Cosbys had some bare walls to cover, they sent for the lot—there were about thirty—and decided to have them cleaned and hang them up. 'After all,' Netta said, 'as well as I can make out through the cobwebs, some of them look like rather jolly copies of early Italian things.' But as she was short of cash she decided to clean them at home instead of sending them to an expert; and one day, while she was operating on this very one before you, with her sleeves rolled up, the man called who always *does* call on such occasions; the man who knows. In the given case, it was a quiet fellow connected with the Louvre, who'd brought her a letter from Paris, and whom she'd invited to one of her stupid dinners. He was announced, and she thought it would be a joke to let him see what she was doing; she has pretty arms, you may remember. So he was asked into the dining-room, where he found her with a pail of hot water and soap-suds, and *this* laid out on the table; and the first thing he did was to grab her pretty arm so tight that it was black and blue, while he shouted out: 'God in heaven! Not *hot* water!'"

My friend leaned back with a sigh of mingled resentment and satisfaction, and we sat silently looking up at the lovely "Adoration" above the mantelpiece.

"That's how I got it a little cheaper—most of the old varnish was gone for good. But luckily for her it was the first picture she had attacked; and as for the others—you must see them, that's all I can say. . . . Wait; I've got the catalogue somewhere about. . . ."

He began to rummage for it, and I asked, remembering how nearly I had married Netta Kent: "Do you mean to say she didn't keep a single one of them?"

"Oh, yes—in the shape of pearls and Rolls-Royces. And you've seen their new house in Fifth Avenue?" He ended with a grin of irony: "The best of the joke is that Jim was just thinking of divorcing her when the pictures were discovered."

"Poor little Louisa!" I sighed.

THE END

The Punctiliousness of Don Sebastian

W. Somerset Maugham

and

View of Toledo

El Greco

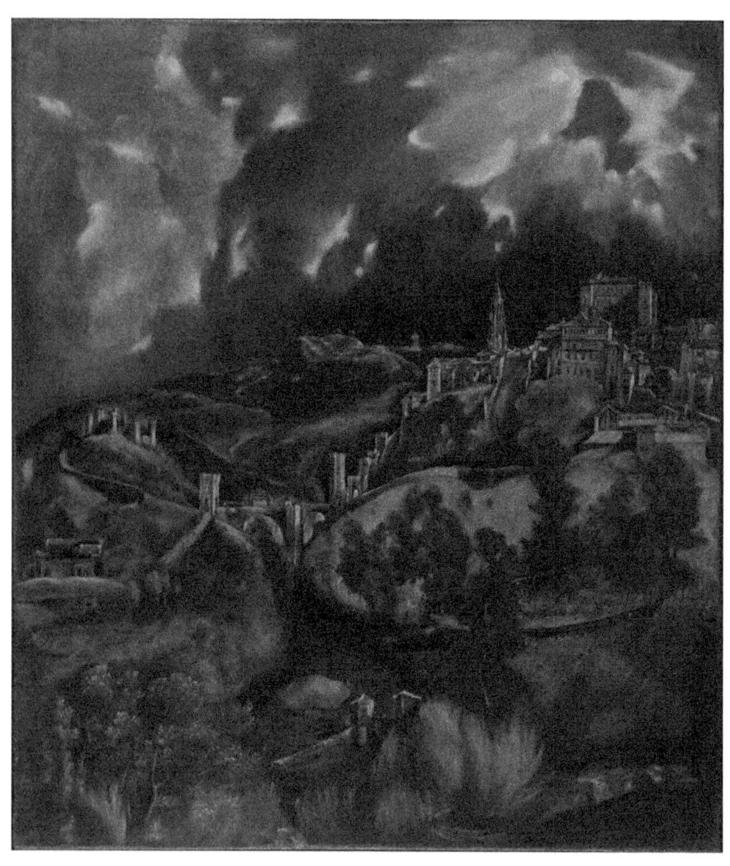

El Greco (Domenikos Theotokopoulos), *View of Toledo* (ca. 1599–1600), H. O. Havemeyer Collection, Bequest of Mrs. H. O. Havemeyer, 1929.

Artists manipulate the landscape that they replicate on canvas just as people invent and reinvent their identities and the narratives that they live out. El Greco's attention to detail in *View of Toledo* enables us to behold the panoramic sweep of his beloved city. His taking the liberty to reposition the cathedral beside the palace brings our horizontal gaze to vertical. The cross atop the spire pierces the sky which churns passionately and darkly above Toledo. Below, the muted lush green flanks the heavy stone architecture. While there are distant signs of human life, the city seems to protect its narratives. W. Somerset Maugham's "The Punctiliousness of Don Sebastian" slowly unwinds hidden stories of the first Duke of Losas, Don Sebastian, revealed by the last representative of the now-insignificant Duchy of Losas. Authentic love, betrayal, grief, revenge, and greed exert their influence on Don Sebastian's identity until his final image is eternalized by his elaborate, alabaster tomb. We meet the isolated Spanish town of Xiormonez shrouded by the whirling, heavy blackness of night as the narrator stumbles through the paths leading to the town while shadows of large crucifixes rise up as he passes. The town itself obscures the sky and its dark windows gape at him while the cathedral's gargoyles loom menacingly like demons as he hurries through this underworld. Cries of the pious punctuate the night at regular intervals, entreating Mary Queen of Heaven for protection. What seems is not always what is. In this crumbling town overshadowed by the gray forbidding cathedral, much of the decorum has hidden debauchery and intrigue. In the end, stone divulges no secrets.

—Ellen Francese

The Punctiliousness of Don Sebastian

W. Somerset Maugham

First published in 1899 in Orientations *by T. Fisher Unwin, London.*

I

Xiormonez is the most inaccessible place in Spain. Only one train arrives there in the course of the day, and that arrives at two o'clock in the morning; only one train leaves it, and that starts an hour before sunrise. No one has ever been able to discover what happens to the railway officials during the intermediate one-and-twenty hours. A German painter I met there, who had come by the only train, and had been endeavouring for a fortnight to get up in time to go away, told me that he had frequently gone to the station in order to clear up the mystery, but had never been able to do so; yet, from his inquiries, he was inclined to suspect—that was as far as he would commit himself, being a cautious man—that they spent the time in eating garlic and smoking execrable cigarettes. The guide-books tell you that Xiormonez possesses the eyebrows of Joseph of Arimathea, a cathedral of the greatest quaintness, and battlements untouched since their erection in the fourteenth century. And they strongly advise you to visit it, but recommend you before doing so to add Keating's insect powder to your other toilet necessaries.

I was travelling to Madrid in an express train which had been rushing along at the pace of sixteen miles an hour, when suddenly it stopped. I leant out of the window, asking where we were.

'Xiormonez!' answered the guard.

'I thought we did not stop at Xiormonez.'

'We do not stop at Xiormonez,' he replied impassively.

'But we are stopping now!'

'That may be; but we are going on again.'

I had already learnt that it was folly to argue with a Spanish guard, and, drawing back my head, I sat down. But, looking at my watch, I saw that it was only ten. I should never again have a chance of inspecting the eyebrows of Joseph of Arimathea unless I chartered a special train, so, seizing the opportunity and my bag, I jumped out.

The only porter told me that everyone in Xiormonez

was asleep at that hour, and recommended me to spend the night in the waiting-room, but I bribed him heavily; I offered him two pesetas, which is nearly fifteenpence, and, leaving the train to its own devices, he shouldered my bag and started off.

Along a stony road we walked into the dark night, the wind blowing cold and bitter, and the clouds chasing one another across the sky. In front, I could see nothing but the porter hurrying along, bent down under the weight of my bag, and the wind blew icily. I buttoned up my coat. And then I regretted the warmth of the carriage, the comfort of my corner and my rug; I wished I had peacefully continued my journey to Madrid—I was on the verge of turning back as I heard the whistling of the train. I hesitated, but the porter hurried on, and fearing to lose him in the night, I sprang forwards. Then the puffing of the engine, and on the smoke the bright reflection of the furnace, and the train steamed away; like Abd-er-Rahman, I felt that I had flung my scabbard into the flames.

Still the porter hurried on, bent down under the weight of my bag, and I saw no light in front of me to announce the approach to a town. On each side, bordering the road, were trees, and beyond them darkness. And great black clouds hastened after one another across the heavens. Then, as we walked along, we came to a rough stone cross, and lying on the steps before it was a woman with uplifted hands. And the wind blew bitter and keen, freezing the marrow of one's bones. What prayers had she to offer that she must kneel there alone in the night? We passed another cross standing up with its outstretched arms like a soul in pain. At last a heavier night rose before me, and presently I saw a great stone arch. Passing beneath it, I found myself immediately in the town.

The street was tortuous and narrow, paved with rough cobbles; and it rose steeply, so that the porter bent lower beneath his burden, panting. With the bag on his shoulders he looked like some hunchbacked gnome, a creature of nightmare. On either side rose tall houses, lying crooked and irregular, leaning towards one another at the top, so that one could not see the clouds, and their windows were great, black apertures like giant mouths. There was not a light, not a soul, not a sound—except that of my own feet and the heavy panting of the porter. We wound through the streets, round corners, through low arches, a long way up the steep cobbles, and suddenly down broken steps. They hurt my feet, and I stumbled and almost fell, but the hunchback walked along nimbly, hurrying ever. Then we came into an open space, and the wind caught us again, and blew through our clothes, so that I shrank up, shivering. And never a soul did we see as we walked on; it might have been a city of the dead. Then past a tall church: I saw a carved porch, and from the side grim devils grinning down upon me; the porter dived through an arch, and I groped my way along a narrow passage. At length he stopped, and with a sigh threw down the bag. He beat with his fists against an iron door, making the metal ring. A window above was thrown open, and a voice cried out. The porter answered; there was a clattering down the stairs, an unlocking, and the door was timidly held open, so that I saw a woman, with the light of her candle throwing a strange yellow glare on her face.

And so I arrived at the hotel of Xiormonez.

II

My night was troubled by the ghostly crying of the watchman: 'Protect us, Mary, Queen of Heaven; protect us, Mary!' Every hour it rang out stridently as soon as the heavy bells of the cathedral had ceased their clanging, and I thought of the woman kneeling at the cross, and wondered if her soul had found peace.

In the morning I threw open the windows and the sun came dancing in, flooding the room with gold. In front of me the great wall of the cathedral stood grim and grey, and the gargoyles looked savagely across the square. . . . The cathedral is admirable; when you enter you find yourself at once in darkness, and the air is heavy with incense; but, as your eyes become accustomed to the gloom, you see the black forms of penitents kneeling by pillars, looking towards an altar, and by the light of the painted windows a reredos, with the gaunt saints of an early painter, and aureoles shining dimly.

But the gem of the Cathedral of Xiormonez is the Chapel of the Duke de Losas, containing, as it does, the alabaster monument of Don Sebastian Emanuel de Mantona, Duque de Losas, and of the very illustrious Señora Doña Sodina de Berruguete, his wife. Like everything else in Spain, the chapel is kept locked up, and the guide-book tells you to apply to the porter at the palace of the present duke. I sent a little boy to fetch that worthy, who presently came back, announcing that the porter and his wife had gone into the country for the day, but that the duke was coming in person.

And immediately I saw walking towards me a little, dark man, wrapped up in a big capa, with the red and blue velvet of the lining flung gaudily over his shoulder. He bowed courteously as he approached, and I perceived that on the crown his hair was somewhat more than thin. I hesitated a little, rather awkwardly, for the guide-book said that the porter exacted a fee of one peseta for opening the chapel—one could scarcely offer sevenpence-halfpenny to a duke. But he quickly put an end to all doubt, for, as he unlocked the door, he turned to me and said,—

'The fee is one franc.'

As I gave it him he put it in his pocket and gravely handed me a little printed receipt. Baedeker had obligingly informed me that the Duchy of Losas was shorn of its splendour, but I had not understood that the present representative added to his income by exhibiting the bones of his ancestors at a franc a head. . . .

We entered, and the duke pointed out the groining of the roof and the tracery of the windows.

'This chapel contains some of the finest Gothic in Spain,' he said.

When he considered that I had sufficiently admired the architecture, he turned to the pictures, and, with the fluency of a professional guide, gave me their subjects and the names of the artists.

'Now we come to the tombs of Don Sebastian, the first Duke of Losas, and his spouse, Doña Sodina—not, however, the first duchess.'

The monument stood in the middle of the chapel, covered with a great pall of red velvet, so that no economical tourist should see it through the bars of the gate and thus save his peseta. The duke removed the covering and watched me silently, a slight smile trembling below his little, black moustache.

The duke and his wife, who was not his duchess, lay side by side on a bed of carved alabaster; at the corners were four twisted pillars, covered with little leaves and flowers, and between them bas-reliefs representing Love, and Youth, and Strength, and Pleasure, as if, even in the midst of death, death must be forgotten. Don Sebastian was in full armour. His helmet was admirably carved with a representation of the battle between the Centaurs and the Lapithæ; on the right arm-piece were portrayed the adventures of Venus and Mars, on the left the emotions of Vulcan; but on the breast-plate was an elaborate Crucifixion, with soldiers and women and apostles. The visor was raised, and showed a stern, heavy face, with prominent cheek bones, sensual lips and a massive chin.

'It is very fine,' I remarked, thinking the duke expected some remark.

'People have thought so for three hundred years,' he replied gravely.

He pointed out to me the hands of Don Sebastian.

'The guide-books have said that they are the finest hands in Spain. Tourists especially admire the tendons and veins, which, as you perceive, stand out as in no human hand would be possible. They say it is the summit of art.'

And he took me to the other side of the monument, that I might look at Doña Sodina.

'They say she was the most beautiful woman of her day,' he said, 'but in that case the Castilian lady is the only thing in Spain which has not degenerated.'

She was, indeed, not beautiful: her face was fat and broad, like her husband's; a short, ungraceful nose, and a little, nobbly chin; a thick neck, set dumpily on her marble shoulders. One could not but hope that the artist had done her an injustice.

The Duke of Losas made me observe the dog which was lying at her feet.

'It is a symbol of fidelity,' he said.

'The guide-book told me she was chaste and faithful.'

'If she had been,' he replied, smiling, 'Don Sebastian would perhaps never have become Duque de Losas.'

'Really!'

'It is an old history which I discovered one day among some family papers.'

I pricked up my ears, and discreetly began to question him.

'Are you interested in old manuscripts?' said the duke. 'Come with me and I will show you what I have.'

With a flourish of the hand he waved me out of the chapel,

and, having carefully locked the doors, accompanied me to his palace. He took me into a Gothic chamber, furnished with worn French furniture, the walls covered with cheap paper. Offering me a cigarette, he opened a drawer and produced a faded manuscript.

'This is the document in question,' he said. 'Those crooked and fantastic characters are terrible. I often wonder if the writers were able to read them.'

'You are fortunate to be the possessor of such things,' I remarked.

He shrugged his shoulders.

'What good are they? I would sooner have fifty pesetas than this musty parchment.'

An offer! I quickly reckoned it out into English money. He would doubtless have taken less, but I felt a certain delicacy in bargaining with a duke over his family secrets....

'Do you mean it? May I—er—'

He sprang towards me.

'Take it, my dear sir, take it. Shall I give you a receipt?'

And so, for thirty-one shillings and threepence, I obtained the only authentic account of how the frailty of the illustrious Señora Doña Sodina was indirectly the means of raising her husband to the highest dignities in Spain.

III

Don Sebastian and his wife had lived together for fifteen years, with the entirest happiness to themselves and the greatest admiration of their neighbours. People said that such an example of conjugal felicity was not often seen in those degenerate days, for even then they prated of the golden age of their grandfathers, lamenting their own decadence. . . . As behoved good Castilians, burdened with such a line of noble ancestors, the fortunate couple conducted themselves with all imaginable gravity. No strange eye was permitted to witness a caress between the lord and his lady, or to hear an expression of endearment; but everyone could see the devotion of Don Sebastian, the look of adoration which filled his eyes when he gazed upon his wife. And people said that Doña Sodina was worthy of all his affection. They said that her virtue was only matched by her piety, and her piety was patent to the whole world, for every day she went to the cathedral at Xiormonez and remained long immersed in her devotions. Her charity was exemplary, and no beggar ever applied to her in vain.

But even if Don Sebastian and his wife had not possessed these conjugal virtues, they would have been in Xiormonez persons of note, since not only did they belong to an old and respected family, which was rich as well, but the gentleman's brother was archbishop of the See, who, when he graced the cathedral city with his presence, paid the greatest attention to Don Sebastian and Doña Sodina. Everyone said that the Archbishop Pablo would shortly become a cardinal, for he was a great favourite with the king, and with the latter His Holiness the Pope was then on terms of quite unusual friendship.

And in those days, when the priesthood was more noticeable for its gallantry than for its good works, it was refreshing to find so high-placed a dignitary of the Church a pattern of Christian virtues, who, notwithstanding his gorgeous habit of life, his retinue, his palaces, recalled, by his freedom from at least two of the seven deadly sins, the simplicity of the apostles, which the common people have often supposed the perfect state of the minister of God.

Don Sebastian had been affianced to Doña Sodina when he was a boy of ten, and before she could properly pronounce the viperish sibilants of her native tongue. When the lady attained her sixteenth year, the pair were solemnly espoused, and the young priest Pablo, the bridegroom's brother, assisted at the ceremony. In these days the union would have been instanced as a triumphant example of the success of the *mariage de convenance*, but at that time such arrangements were so usual that it never occurred to anyone to argue for or against them. Yet it was not customary for a young man of two-and-twenty to fall madly in love with the bride whom he saw for the first time a day or two before his marriage, and it was still less customary for the bride to give back an equal affection. For fifteen years the couple lived in harmony and contentment, with nothing to trouble the even tenor of their lives; and if there was a cloud in their sky, it was that a kindly Providence had vouchsafed no fruit to the union, notwithstanding the prayers and candles which Doña Sodina was known to have offered at the shrine of more than one saint in Spain who had made that kind of miracle particularly his own.

But even felicitous marriages cannot last for ever, since if the love does not die the lovers do. And so it came to pass that Doña Sodina, having eaten excessively of pickled shrimps, which the abbess of a highly respected convent had assured her were of great efficacy in the begetting of children, took a fever of the stomach, as the chronicle inelegantly puts it, and after a week of suffering was called to the other world, from which, as from the pickled shrimps, she had always expected much. There let us hope her virtues have been rewarded, and she rests in peace and happiness.

IV

When Don Sebastian walked from the cathedral to his house after the burial of his wife, no one saw a trace of emotion on his face, and it was with his wonted grave courtesy that he bowed to a friend as he passed him. Sternly and briefly, as usual, he gave orders that no one should disturb him, and went to the room of Doña Sodina; he knelt on the praying-stool which Doña Sodina had daily used for so many years, and he fixed his eyes on the crucifix hanging on the wall above it. The day passed, and the night passed, and Don Sebastian never moved—no thought or emotion entered him; being alive, he was like the dead; he was like the dead that linger on the outer limits of hell, with never a hope for the future, dull with the despair that shall last for ever and ever and ever. But when the woman who had nursed him in his childhood lovingly disobeyed his order and entered to give him food, she saw no tear in his eye, no sign of weeping.

'You are right!' he said, painfully rising from his knees. 'Give me to eat.'

Listlessly taking the food, he sank into a chair and looked at the bed on which had lately rested the corpse of Doña Sodina; but a kindly nature relieved his unhappiness, and he fell into a weary sleep.

When he awoke, the night was far advanced; the house, the town were filled with silence; all round him was darkness, and the ivory crucifix shone dimly, dimly. Outside the door a page was sleeping; he woke him and bade him bring light. . . . In his sorrow, Don Sebastian began to look at the things his wife had loved; he fingered her rosary, and turned over the pages of the half-dozen pious books which formed her library; he looked at the jewels which he had seen glittering on her bosom; the brocades, the rich silks, the cloths of gold and silver that she had delighted to wear. And at last he came across an old breviary which he thought she had lost—how glad she would have been to find it, she had so often regretted it! The pages were musty with their long concealment, and only faintly could be detected the scent which Doña Sodina used yearly to make and strew about her things. Turning over the pages listlessly, he saw some crabbed writing; he took it to the light—'*To-night, my beloved, I come.*' And the handwriting was that of Pablo, Archbishop of Xiormonez. Don Sebastian looked at it long. Why should his brother write such words in the breviary of Doña Sodina? He turned the pages and the handwriting of his wife met his eye and the words were the same—'*To-night, my beloved, I come'*—as if they were such delight to her that she must write them herself. The breviary dropped from Don Sebastian's hand.

The taper, flickering in the draught, threw glaring lights on Don Sebastian's face, but it showed no change in it. He sat looking at the fallen breviary, and, in his mind, at the love which was dead. At last he passed his hand over his forehead.

'And yet,' he whispered, 'I loved thee well!'

But as the day came he picked up the breviary and locked it in a casket; he knelt again at the praying-stool and, lifting his hands to the crucifix, prayed silently. Then he locked the door of Doña Sodina's room, and it was a year before he entered it again.

That day the Archbishop Pablo came to his brother to offer consolation for his loss, and Don Sebastian at the parting kissed him on either cheek.

V

The people of Xiormonez said that Don Sebastian was heart-broken, for from the date of his wife's interment he was not seen in the streets by day. A few, returning home from some riot, had met him wandering in the dead of the night, but he passed them silently by. But he sent his servants to Toledo and Burgos, to Salamanca, Cordova, even to Paris and Rome; and from all these places they brought him books—and day after day he studied in them, till the common folk asked if he had turned magician.

So passed eleven months, and nearly twelve, till it wanted but five days to the anniversary of the death of Doña Sodina. Then Don Sebastian wrote to his brother the letter which for months he had turned over in his mind,—

'Seeing the instability of all human things, and the uncertain length of our exile upon earth, I have considered that it is evil for brothers to remain so separate. Therefore I implore you—who are my only relative in this world, and heir to all my goods and estates—to visit me quickly, for I have a presentiment that death is not far off, and I would see you before we are parted by the immense sea.'

The archbishop was thinking that he must shortly pay a visit to his cathedral city, and, as his brother had desired, came to Xiormonez immediately. On the anniversary of Doña Sodina's interment, Don Sebastian entertained Archbishop Pablo to supper.

'My brother,' said he, to his guest, 'I have lately received from Cordova a wine which I desire you to taste. It is very highly prized in Africa, whence I am told it comes, and it is made with curious art and labour.'

Glass cups were brought, and the wine poured in. The archbishop was a connoisseur, and held it between the light and himself, admiring the sparkling clearness, and then inhaled the odour.

'It is nectar,' he said.

At last he sipped it.

'The flavour is very strange.'

He drank deeply. Don Sebastian looked at him and smiled as his brother put down the empty glass. But when he was himself about to drink, the cup fell between his hands and the steward's, breaking into a hundred fragments, and the wine spilt on the floor.

'Fool!' cried Don Sebastian, and in his anger struck the servant.

But being a man of peace, the archbishop interposed.

'Do not be angry with him; it was an accident. There is more wine in the flagon.'

'No, I will not drink it,' said Don Sebastian, wrathfully. 'I will drink no more to-night.'

The archbishop shrugged his shoulders.

When they were alone, Don Sebastian made a strange request.

'My brother, it is a year to-day that Sodina was buried, and I have not entered her room since then. But now I have a desire to see it. Will you come with me?'

The archbishop consented, and together they crossed the long corridor that led to Doña Sodina's apartment, preceded by a boy with lights.

Don Sebastian unlocked the door, and, taking the taper from the page's hand, entered. The archbishop followed. The air was chill and musty, and even now an odour of recent death seemed to pervade the room.

Don Sebastian went to a casket, and from it took a breviary. He saw his brother start as his eye fell on it. He turned over the leaves till he came to a page on which was the archbishop's handwriting, and handed it to him.

'Oh God!' exclaimed the priest, and looked quickly at the door. Don Sebastian was standing in front of it. He opened his mouth to cry out, but Don Sebastian interrupted him.

'Do not be afraid! I will not touch you.'

For a while they looked at one another silently; one pale, sweating with terror, the other calm and grave as usual. At last Don Sebastian spoke, hoarsely.

'Did she—did she love you?'

'Oh, my brother, forgive her. It was long ago—and she repented bitterly. And I—I!'

'I have forgiven you.'

The words were said so strangely that the archbishop shuddered. What did he mean?

Don Sebastian smiled.

'You have no cause for anxiety. From now it is finished. I will forget.' And, opening the door, he helped his brother across the threshold. The archbishop's hand was clammy as a hand of death.

When Don Sebastian bade his brother good-night, he kissed him on either cheek.

VI

The priest returned to his palace, and when he was in bed his secretary prepared to read to him, as was his wont, but the archbishop sent him away, desiring to be alone. He tried to think; but the wine he had drunk was heavy upon him, and he fell asleep. But presently he awoke, feeling thirsty; he drank some water. . . . Then he became strangely wide-awake, a feeling of uneasiness came over him as of some threatening presence behind him, and again he felt the thirst. He stretched out his hand for the flagon, but now there was a mist before his eyes and he could not see, his hand trembled so that he spilled the water. And the uneasiness was magnified till it became a terror, and the thirst was horrible. He opened his mouth to call out, but his throat was dry, so that no sound came. He tried to rise from his bed, but his limbs were heavy and he could not move. He breathed quicker and quicker, and his skin was extraordinarily dry. The terror became an agony; it was unbearable. He wanted to bury his face in the pillows to hide it from him; he felt the hair on his head hard and dry, and it stood on end! He called to God for help, but no sound came from his mouth. Then the terror took shape and form, and he knew that behind him was standing Doña Sodina, and she was looking at him with terrible, reproachful eyes. And a second Doña Sodina came and stood at the end of the bed, and another came by her side, and the room was filled with them. And his thirst was horrible; he tried to moisten his mouth with spittle, but the source of it was dry. Cramps seized his limbs, so that he writhed with pain. Presently a red glow fell upon the room and it became hot and hotter, till he gasped for breath; it blinded him, but he could not close his eyes. And he knew it was the glow of hell-fire, for in his ears rang the groans of souls in torment, and among the voices he recognised that of Doña Sodina, and then—then he heard his own voice. And, in the livid heat, he saw himself in his episcopal robes, lying on the ground, chained to Doña Sodina, hand and foot. And he knew that as long as heaven and earth should last, the torment of hell would continue.

When the priests came in to their master in the morning, they found him lying dead, with his eyes wide open, staring with a ghastly brilliancy into the unknown. Then there was weeping and lamentation, and from house to house the people told one another that the archbishop had died in his sleep. The bells were set tolling, and as Don Sebastian, in his solitude, heard them, referring to the chief ingredient of that strange wine from Cordova, he permitted himself the only jest of his life.

'It was *Belladonna* that sent his body to the worms; and it was *Belladonna* that sent his soul to hell.'

VII

The chronicle does not state whether the thought of his brother's heritage had ever entered Don Sebastian's head; but the fact remains that he was sole heir, and the archbishop had gathered the loaves and fishes to such purpose during his life that his death made Don Sebastian one of the wealthiest men in Spain. The simplest actions in this world, oh Martin Tupper! have often the most unforeseen results.

Now, Don Sebastian had always been ambitious, and his changed circumstances made him realise more clearly than ever that his merit was worthy of a brilliant arena. The times were propitious, for the old king had just died, and the new one had sent away the army of priests and monks which had turned every day into a Sunday; people said that God Almighty had had His day, and that the heathen deities had come to rule in His stead. From all corners of Spain gallants were coming to enjoy the sunshine, and everyone who could make a compliment or a graceful bow was sure of a welcome.

So Don Sebastian prepared to go to Madrid. But before leaving his native town he thought well to appease a possibly vengeful Providence by erecting in the cathedral a chapel in honour of his patron saint; not that he thought the saints would trouble themselves about the death of his brother, even though the causes of it were not entirely natural, but Don Sebastian remembered that Pablo was an archbishop, and the fact caused him a certain anxiety. He called together architects and sculptors, and ordered them to erect an edifice befitting his dignity; and being a careful man, as all Spaniards are, thought he would serve himself as well as the saint, and bade the sculptors make an image of Doña Sodina and an image of himself, in order that he might use the chapel also as a burial-place.

To pay for this, Don Sebastian left the revenue of several of his brother's farms, and then, with a peaceful conscience, set out for the capital.

At Madrid he laid himself out to gain the favour of his sovereign, and by dint of unceasing flattery soon received much of the king's attention; and presently Philip deigned to ask his advice on petty matters. And since Don Sebastian took care to advise as he saw the king desired, the latter concluded that the courtier was a man of stamina and ability, and began to consult him on matters of state.

Don Sebastian opined that the pleasure of the prince must always come before the welfare of the nation, and the king was so impressed with his sagacity that one day he asked his opinion on a question of precedence—to the indignation of the most famous councillors in the land.

But the haughty soul of Don Sebastian chafed because he was only one among many favourites. The court was full of flatterers as assiduous and as obsequious as himself; his proud Castilian blood could brook no companions. . . . But one day, as he was moodily waiting in the royal antechamber, thinking of these things, it occurred to him that a certain profession had always been in great honour among princes, and he remembered that he had a cousin of eighteen, who was being educated in a convent near Xiormonez. She was beautiful. With buoyant heart he went to his house and told his steward to fetch her from the convent at once. Within a fortnight she was at Madrid. . . . Mercia was presented to the queen in the presence of Philip, and Don Sebastian noticed that the royal eye lighted up as he gazed on the bashful maiden. Then all the proud Castilian had to do was to shut his eyes and allow the king to make his own opportunities. Within a week Mercia was created maid of honour to the queen, and Don Sebastian was seized with an indisposition which confined him to his room.

The king paid his court royally, which is, boldly; and Doña Mercia had received in the convent too religious an education not to know that it was her duty to grant the king whatever it graciously pleased him to ask. . . .

When Don Sebastian recovered from his illness, he found the world at his feet, for everyone was talking of the king's new mistress, and it was taken as a matter of course that her cousin and guardian should take a prominent part in the affairs of the country. But Don Sebastian was furious! He went to the king and bitterly reproached him for thus dishonouring him. . . . Philip was a humane and generous-minded man, and understood that with a certain temperament it might be annoying to have one's ward philander with a king, so he did his best to console the courtier. He called him his friend and brother; he told him he would always love him, but Don Sebastian would not be consoled. And nothing would comfort him except to be made High Admiral of the Fleet. Philip was charmed to settle the matter so simply, and as he delighted in generosity when to be generous cost him nothing, he also created Don Sebastian Duke of Losas, and gave him, into the bargain, the hand of the richest heiress in Spain.

And that is the end of the story of the punctiliousness of Don Sebastian. With his second wife he lived many years, beloved of his sovereign, courted by the world, honoured by all, till he was visited by the Destroyer of Delights and the Leveller of the Grandeur of this World. . . .

VIII

Towards evening, the Duke of Losas passed my hotel, and, seeing me at the door, asked if I had read the manuscript.

'I thought it interesting,' I said, a little coldly, for, of course, I knew no Englishman would have acted like Don Sebastian.

He shrugged his shoulders.

'It is not half so interesting as a good dinner.'

At these words I felt bound to offer him such hospitality as the hotel afforded. I found him a very agreeable mess-mate. He told me the further history of his family, which nearly became extinct at the end of the last century, since the only son of the seventh duke had, unfortunately, not been born of any duchess. But Ferdinand, who was then King of Spain, was unwilling that an ancient family should die out, and was, at the same time, sorely in want of money; so the titles and honours of the house were continued to the son of the seventh duke, and King Ferdinand built himself another palace.

'But now,' said my guest, mournfully shaking his head, 'it is finished. My palace and a few acres of barren rock are all that remain to me of the lands of my ancestors, and I am the last of the line.'

But I bade him not despair. He was a bachelor and a duke, and not yet forty. I advised him to go to the United States before they put a duty on foreign noblemen; this was before the war; and I recommended him to take Maida Vale and Manchester on his way. Personally, I gave him a letter of introduction to an heiress of my acquaintance at Hampstead; for even in these days it is not so bad a thing to be Duchess of Losas, and the present duke has no brother.

De Amicitia

W. Somerset Maugham

and

Marie Joséphine Charlotte du Val d'Ognes

Marie Denise Villers

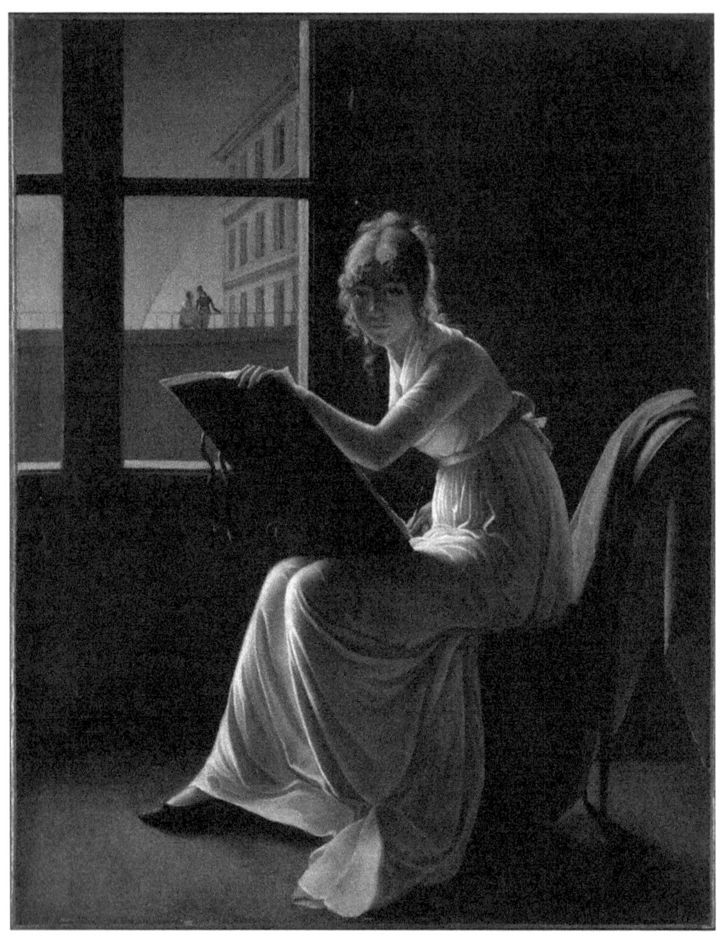

Marie Denise Villers, *Marie Joséphine Charlotte du Val d'Ognes* (1801), Mr. and Mrs. Isaac D. Fletcher Collection, Bequest of Isaac D. Fletcher, 1917.

How do women navigate passion and love? Historically men have been free to love without consequence, yet women risk everything if they reject society's guiding virtues of proper conduct. On the other hand, they are told that sustaining a friendship with a man is impossible, even if the man agrees to abide by the boundaries. Artists often use their passion to describe the world through their lens, yet the authenticity of expression of female artists has too often been curtailed. In *Marie Joséphine Charlotte du Val d'Ognes*, Marie Denise Villers candidly paints a portrait of a young female artist who seems to be gazing at Villers and at us. The eyes engage us but remain distant, her slender fingers loosely holding her brush. Her light, draping dress clings to her, revealing the contours of her lithe body. Though her golden hair is pulled up, rogue curls frame her face and dangle like sunlit waves along her neck. Her pale skin glows softly in shafts of sunlight that enter the room. While we cannot see her canvas, what we do spy is a pair of lovers leaning on a railing at a distance outside the window behind the young painter. The window functions as a second painting. Another glance reveals a jagged edge of broken glass. No window pane divides us from the couple outside. Perhaps we wonder about the girl's vulnerability, as nothing separates the lovers from her. The window acts as a portrait of possibility, one still shielded from the girl by the remaining sharp-edged shard of glass. Finally, we may return to wondering what she is painting and why she keeps it safe from the viewer's glance. W. Somerset Maugham's "De Amicitia" follows a story of a young female painter and a young male poet. Like the girl in Viller's portrait, Valentia lives divided from love's passion. Early on, the young artists laud Plato who rejects the common Aphrodite. The pact Valentia makes with Ferdinand fills her with joy sprung from a shared value of friendship that opposes the desires of the body. As the story's name suggests, the young artists subscribe to Cicero's treatise of the same title which states that virtue provides the foundation for true friendship. The world of Valentia and Ferdinand is a delicate one, contained by an invisible barrier much like the pane of glass in the painting. From the beginning, we hear voices that question the possibility and value of sustaining a friendship impinging on the thin glass that shields the friends from the fullness of life and from what lies within themselves. The young artists take great pride in the praiseworthy purity of their friendship. For Valentia, this relationship not only strengthens her but also releases her from the fetters of her gender. However, throughout the narrative their mutual attraction slowly emerges. As they stand in silence, the mute, deep darkness of night enfolds them in mystery, an alchemist stirring the senses. Finally, it is the shared wonder of the sunlit, vital landscape colored by their open avowals of love that enlarges their capacity to feel the extraordinariness of daily life, thus released from their previous intellectual shackles. We may wonder if the painter in the Villers portrait will turn her gaze to the lovers outside her window, perhaps translating what she sees and feels onto her blank canvas.

—Ellen Francese

De Amicitia

W. Somerset Maugham

First published in 1899 in Orientations *by Fisher Unwin, London.*

I

They were walking home from the theatre.

'Well, Mr White,' said Valentia, 'I think it was just fine.'

'It was magnificent!' replied Mr White.

And they were separated for a moment by the crowd, streaming up from the Français towards the Opera and the Boulevards.

'I think, if you don't mind,' she said, 'I'll take your arm, so that we shouldn't get lost.'

He gave her his arm, and they walked through the Louvre and over the river on their way to the Latin Quarter.

Valentia was an art student and Ferdinand White was a poet. Ferdinand considered Valentia the only woman who had ever been able to paint, and Valentia told Ferdinand that he was the only man she had met who knew anything about Art without being himself an artist. On her arrival in Paris, a year before, she had immediately inscribed herself, at the offices of the *New York Herald*, Valentia Stewart, Cincinnati, Ohio, U.S.A. She settled down in a respectable *pension*, and within a week was painting vigorously. Ferdinand White arrived from Oxford at about the same time, hired a dirty room in a shabby hotel, ate his meals at cheap restaurants in the Boulevard St Michel, read Stephen Mallarmé, and flattered himself that he was leading '*la vie de Bohême*.'

After two months, the Fates brought the pair together, and Ferdinand began to take his meals at Valentia's *pension*. They went to the museums together; and in the Sculpture Gallery at the Louvre, Ferdinand would discourse on ancient Greece in general and on Plato in particular, while among the pictures Valentia would lecture on tones and values and chiaroscuro. Ferdinand renounced Ruskin and all his works; Valentia read the Symposium. Frequently in the evening they went to the theatre; sometimes to the Français, but more often to the Odéon; and after the performance they would discuss the play, its art, its technique—above all, its ethics. Ferdinand explained the piece he had in contemplation, and Valentia talked of the picture she meant to paint for next year's Salon; and the lady told her friends that her companion was the cleverest man she had met in her life, while he told his that she was the only really sympathetic and intelligent girl he had ever known. Thus were united in bonds of amity, Great Britain on the one side and the United States of America and Ireland on the other.

But when Ferdinand spoke of Valentia to the few Frenchmen he knew, they asked him,—

'But this Miss Stewart—is she pretty?'

'Certainly—in her American way; a long face, with the hair parted in the middle and hanging over the nape of the neck. Her mouth is quite classic.'

'And have you never kissed the classic mouth?'

'I? Never!'

'Has she a good figure?'

'Admirable!'

'And yet—Oh, you English!' And they smiled and shrugged their shoulders as they said, 'How English!'

'But, my good fellow,' cried Ferdinand, in execrable French, 'you don't understand. We are friends, the best of friends.'

They shrugged their shoulders more despairingly than ever.

II

They stood on the bridge and looked at the water and the dark masses of the houses on the Latin side, with the twin towers of Notre Dame rising dimly behind them. Ferdinand thought of the Thames at night, with the barges gliding slowly down, and the twinkling of the lights along the Embankment.

'It must be a little like that in Holland,' she said, 'but without the lights and with greater stillness.'

'When do you start?'

She had been making preparations for spending the summer in a little village near Amsterdam, to paint.

'I can't go now,' cried Valentia. 'Corrie Sayles is going home, and there's no one else I can go with. And I can't go alone. Where are you going?'

'I? I have no plans. . . . I never make plans.'

They paused, looking at the reflections in the water. Then she said,—

'I don't see why you shouldn't come to Holland with me!'

He did not know what to think; he knew she had been reading the Symposium.

'After all,' she said, 'there's no reason why one shouldn't go away with a man as well as with a woman.'

His French friends would have suggested that there were many reasons why one should go away with a woman rather than a man; but, like his companion, Ferdinand looked at it in the light of pure friendship.

'When one comes to think of it, I really don't see why we shouldn't. And the mere fact of staying at the same hotel can make no difference to either of us. We shall both have our work—you your painting, and I my play.'

As they considered it, the idea was distinctly pleasing; they wondered that it had not occurred to them before. Sauntering homewards, they discussed the details, and in half an hour had decided on the plan of their journey, the date and the train.

Next day Valentia went to say good-bye to the old French painter whom all the American girls called Popper. She found him in a capacious dressing-gown, smoking cigarettes.

'Well, my dear,' he said, 'what news?'

'I'm going to Holland to paint windmills.'

'A very laudable ambition. With your mother?'

'My good Popper, my mother's in Cincinnati. I'm going with Mr White.'

'With Mr White?' He raised his eyebrows. 'You are very frank about it.'

'Why—what do you mean?'

He put on his glasses and looked at her carefully.

'Does it not seem to you a rather—curious thing for a young girl of your age to go away with a young man of the age of Mr Ferdinand White?'

'Good gracious me! One would think I was doing something that had never been done before!'

'Oh, many a young man has gone travelling with a young woman, but they generally start by a night train, and arrive at the station in different cabs.'

'But surely, Popper, you don't mean to insinuate—Mr White and I are going to Holland as friends.'

'Friends!'

He looked at her more curiously than ever.

'One can have a man friend as well as a girl friend,' she continued. 'And I don't see why he shouldn't be just as good a friend.'

'The danger is that he become too good.'

'You misunderstand me entirely, Popper; we are friends, and nothing but friends.'

'You are entirely off your head, my child.'

'Ah! you're a Frenchman, you can't understand these things. We are different.'

'I imagine that you are human beings, even though England and America respectively had the intense good fortune of seeing your birth.'

'We're human beings—and more than that, we're nineteenth century human beings. Love is not everything. It is a part of one—perhaps the lower part—an accessory to man's life, needful for the continuation of the species.'

'You use such difficult words, my dear.'

'There is something higher and nobler and purer than love—there is friendship. Ferdinand White is my friend. I have the amplest confidence in him. I am certain that no unclean thought has ever entered his head.'

She spoke quite heatedly, and as she flushed up, the old painter thought her astonishingly handsome. Then she added as an afterthought,—

'We despise passion. Passion is ugly; it is grotesque.'

The painter stroked his imperial and faintly smiled.

'My child, you must permit me to tell you that you are foolish. Passion is the most lovely thing in the world; without it we should not paint beautiful pictures. It is passion that makes a woman of a society lady; it is passion that makes a man even of—an art critic.'

'We do not want it,' she said. 'We worship Venus Urania. We are all spirit and soul.'

'You have been reading Plato; soon you will read Zola.'

He smiled again, and lit another cigarette.

'Do you disapprove of my going?' she asked after a little silence.

He paused and looked at her. Then he shrugged his shoulders.

'On the contrary, I approve. It is foolish, but that is no reason why you should not do it. After all, folly is the great attribute of man. No judge is as grave as an owl; no soldier fighting for his country flies as rapidly as the hare. You may be strong, but you are not so strong as a horse; you may be gluttonous, but you cannot eat like a boa-constrictor. But there is no beast that can be as foolish as man. And since one should always do what one can do best—be foolish. Strive for folly above all things. Let the height of your ambition be the pointed cap with the golden bells. So, *bon voyage*! I will come and see you off to-morrow.'

The painter arrived at the station with a box of sweets, which he handed to Valentia with a smile. He shook Ferdinand's hand warmly and muttered under his breath,—

'Silly fool! he's thinking of friendship, too!'

Then, as the train steamed out, he waved his hand and cried,—

'Be foolish! Be foolish!'

He walked slowly out of the station, and sat down at a *café*. He lit a cigarette, and, sipping his absinthe, said,—

'Imbeciles!'

III

They arrived at Amsterdam in the evening, and, after dinner, gathered together their belongings and crossed the Ij as the moon shone over the waters; then they got into the little steam tram and started for Monnickendam. They stood side by side on the platform of the carriage and watched the broad meadows bathed in moonlight, the formless shapes of the cattle lying on the grass, and the black outlines of the mills; they passed by a long, sleeping canal, and they stopped at little, silent villages. At last they entered the dead town, and the tram put them down at the hotel door.

Next morning, when she was half dressed, Valentia threw open the window of her room, and looked out into the garden. Ferdinand was walking about, dressed as befitted the place and season—in flannels—with a huge white hat on his head. She could not help thinking him very handsome—and she took off the blue skirt she had intended to work in, and put on a dress of muslin all bespattered with coloured flowers, and she took in her hand a flat straw hat with red ribbons.

'You look like a Dresden shepherdess,' he said, as they met.

They had breakfast in the garden beneath the trees; and as she poured out his tea, she laughed, and with the American accent which he was beginning to think made English so harmonious, said,—

'I reckon this about takes the shine out of Paris.'

They had agreed to start work at once, losing no time, for they wanted to have a lot to show on their return to France, that their scheme might justify itself. Ferdinand wished to accompany Valentia on her search for the picturesque, but she would not let him; so, after breakfast, he sat himself down in the summer-house, and spread out all round him his nice white paper, lit his pipe, cut his quills, and proceeded to the evolution of a masterpiece. Valentia tied the red strings of her sun-bonnet under her chin, selected a sketchbook, and sallied forth.

At luncheon they met, and Valentia told of a little bit of canal, with an old windmill on one side of it, which she had decided to paint, while Ferdinand announced that he had settled on the names of his *dramatis personæ*. In the afternoon they returned to their work, and at night, tired with the previous day's travelling, went to bed soon after dinner.

So passed the second day; and the third day, and the fourth; till the end of the week came, and they had worked diligently. They were both of them rather surprised at the ease with which they became accustomed to their life.

'How absurd all this fuss is,' said Valentia, 'that people make about the differences of the sexes! I am sure it is only habit.'

'We have ourselves to prove that there is nothing in it,' he replied. 'You know, it is an interesting experiment that we are making.'

She had not looked at it in that light before.

'Perhaps it is. We may be the fore-runners of a new era.'

'The Edisons of a new communion!'

'I shall write and tell Monsieur Rollo all about it.'

In the course of the letter, she said,—

'Sex is a morbid instinct. Out here, in the calmness of the canal and the broad meadows, it never enters one's head. I do not think of Ferdinand as a man—'

She looked up at him as she wrote the words. He was reading a book and she saw him in profile, with the head bent down. Through the leaves the sun lit up his face with a soft light that was almost green, and it occurred to her that it would be interesting to paint him.

'I do not think of Ferdinand as a man; to me he is a companion. He has a wider experience than a woman, and he talks of different things. Otherwise I see no difference. On his part, the idea of my sex never occurs to him, and far from being annoyed as an ordinary woman might be, I am proud of it. It shows me that, when I chose a companion, I chose well. To him I am not a woman; I am a man.'

And she finished with a repetition of Ferdinand's remark,—

'We are the Edisons of a new communion!'

When Valentia began to paint her companion's portrait, they were naturally much more together. And they never grew tired of sitting in the pleasant garden under the trees, while she worked at her canvas and green shadows fell on the profile of Ferdinand White. They talked of many things. After a while they became less reserved about their private concerns. Valentia told Ferdinand about her home in Ohio, and about her people; and Ferdinand spoke of the country parsonage in which he had spent his childhood, and the public school, and lastly of Oxford and the strange, happy days when he had learnt to read Plato and Walter Pater. . . .

At last Valentia threw aside her brushes and leant back with a sigh.

'It is finished!'

Ferdinand rose and stretched himself, and went to look at his portrait. He stood before it for a while, and then he placed his hand on Valentia's shoulder.

'You are a genius, Miss Stewart.'

She looked up at him.

'Ah, Mr White, I was inspired by you. It is more your work than mine.'

IV

In the evening they went out for a stroll. They wandered through the silent street; in the darkness they lost the quaintness of the red brick houses, contrasting with the bright yellow of the paving, but it was even quieter than by day. The street was very broad, and it wound about from east to west and from west to east, and at last it took them to the tiny harbour. Two fishing smacks were basking on the water, moored to the side, and the Zuyder Zee was covered with the innumerable reflections of the stars. On one of the boats a man was sitting at the prow, fishing, and now and then, through the darkness, one saw the red glow of his pipe; by his side, huddled up on a sail, lay a sleeping boy. The other boat seemed deserted. Ferdinand and Valentia stood for a long time watching the fisher, and he was so still that they wondered whether he too were sleeping. They looked across the sea, and in the distance saw the dim lights of Marken, the island of fishers. They wandered on again through the street, and now the lights in the windows were extinguished one by one, and sleep came over the town; and the quietness was even greater than before. They walked on, and their footsteps made no sound. They felt themselves alone in the dead city, and they did not speak.

At length they came to a canal gliding towards the sea; they followed it inland, and here the darkness was equal to the silence. Great trees that had been planted when William of Orange was king in England threw their shade over the water, shutting out the stars. They wandered along on the soft earth, they could not hear themselves walk—and they did not speak.

They came to a bridge over the canal and stood on it, looking at the water and the trees above them, and the water and the trees below them—and they did not speak.

Then out of the darkness came another darkness, and gradually loomed forth the heaviness of a barge. Noiselessly it glided down the stream, very slowly; at the end of it a boy stood at the tiller, steering; and it passed beneath them and beyond, till it lost itself in the night, and again they were alone.

They stood side by side, leaning against the parapet, looking down at the water. . . . And from the water rose up Love, and Love fluttered down from the trees, and Love was borne along upon the night air. Ferdinand did not know what was happening to him; he felt Valentia by his side, and he drew closer to her, till her dress touched his legs and the silk of her sleeve rubbed against his arm. It was so dark that he could not see her face; he wondered of what she was thinking. She made a little movement and to him came a faint wave of the scent she wore. Presently two forms passed by on the bank and they saw a lover with his arm round a girl's waist, and then they too were hidden in the darkness. Ferdinand trembled as he spoke.

'Only Love is waking!'

'And we!' she said.

'And—you!'

He wondered why she said nothing. Did she understand? He put his hand on her arm.

'Valentia!'

He had never called her by her Christian name before. She turned her face towards him.

'What do you mean?'

'Oh, Valentia, I love you! I can't help it.'

A sob burst from her.

'Didn't you understand,' he said, 'all those hours that I sat for you while you painted, and these long nights in which we wandered by the water?'

'I thought you were my friend.'

'I thought so too. When I sat before you and watched

you paint, and looked at your beautiful hair and your eyes, I thought I was your friend. And I looked at the lines of your body beneath your dress. And when it pleased me to carry your easel and walk with you, I thought it was friendship. Only to-night I know I am in love. Oh, Valentia, I am so glad!'

She could not keep back her tears. Her bosom heaved, and she wept.

'You are a woman,' he said. 'Did you not see?'

'I am so sorry,' she said, her voice all broken. 'I thought we were such good friends. I was so happy. And now you have spoilt it all.'

'Valentia, I love you.'

'I thought our friendship was so good and pure. And I felt so strong in it. It seemed to me so beautiful.'

'Did you think I was less a man than the fisherman you see walking beneath the trees at night?'

'It is all over now,' she sighed.

'What do you mean?'

'I can't stay here with you alone.'

'You're not going away?'

'Before, there was no harm in our being together at the hotel; but now—'

'Oh, Valentia, don't leave me. I can't—I can't live without you.'

She heard the unhappiness in his voice. She turned to him again and laid her two hands on his shoulders.

'Why can't you forget it all, and let us be good friends again? Forget that you are a man. A woman can remain with a man for ever, and always be content to walk and read and talk with him, and never think of anything else. Can you forget it, Ferdinand? You will make me so happy.'

He did not answer, and for a long time they stood on the bridge in silence. At last he sighed—a heartbroken sigh.

'Perhaps you're right. It may be better to pretend that we are friends. If you like, we will forget all this.'

Her heart was too full; she could not answer; but she held out her hands to him. He took them in his own, and, bending down, kissed them.

Then they walked home, side by side, without speaking.

V

Next morning Valentia received M. Rollo's answer to her letter. He apologised for his delay in answering.

'You are a philosopher,' he said—she could see the little snigger with which he had written the words—'You are a philosopher, and I was afraid lest my reply should disturb the course of your reflections on friendship. I confess that I did not entirely understand your letter, but I gathered that the sentiments were correct, and it gave me great pleasure to know that your experiment has had such excellent results. I gather that you have not yet discovered that there is more than a verbal connection between Friendship and Love.'

The reference is to the French equivalents of those states of mind.

'But to speak seriously, dear child. You are young and beautiful now, but not so very many years shall pass before your lovely skin becomes coarse and muddy, and your teeth yellow, and the wrinkles appear about your mouth and eyes. You have not so very many years before you in which to collect sensations, and the recollection of one's loves is, perhaps, the greatest pleasure left to one's old age. To be virtuous, my dear, is admirable, but there are so many interpretations of virtue. For myself, I can say that I have never regretted the temptations to which I succumbed, but often the temptations I have resisted. Therefore, love, love, love! And remember that if love at sixty in a man is sometimes pathetic, in a woman at forty it is always ridiculous. Therefore, take your youth in both hands and say to yourself, "Life is short, but let me live before I die!"'

She did not show the letter to Ferdinand.

Next day it rained. Valentia retired to a room at the top of the house and began to paint, but the incessant patter on the roof got on her nerves; the painting bored her, and she threw aside the brushes in disgust. She came downstairs and found Ferdinand in the dining-room, standing at the window looking at the rain. It came down in one continual steady pour, and the water ran off the raised brickwork of the middle of the street to the gutters by the side, running along in a swift and murky rivulet. The red brick of the opposite house looked cold and cheerless in the wet. . . . He did not turn or speak to her as she came in. She remarked that it did not look like leaving off. He made no answer. She drew a chair to the second window and tried to read, but she could not understand what she was reading. And she looked out at the pouring rain and the red brick house opposite. She wondered why he had not answered.

The innkeeper brought them their luncheon. Ferdinand took no notice of the preparations.

'Will you come to luncheon, Mr White?' she said to him. 'It is quite ready.'

'I beg your pardon,' he said gravely, as he took his seat.

He looked at her quickly, and then immediately dropping his eyes, began eating. She wished he would not look so sad; she was very sorry for him.

She made an observation and he appeared to rouse himself. He replied and they began talking, very calmly and coldly, as if they had not known one another five minutes. They talked of Art with the biggest of A's, and they compared Dutch painting with Italian; they spoke of Rembrandt and his life.

'Rembrandt had passion,' said Ferdinand, bitterly, 'and therefore he was unhappy. It is only the sexless, passionless creature, the block of ice, that can be happy in this world.'

She blushed and did not answer.

The afternoon Valentia spent in her room, pretending to write letters, and she wondered whether Ferdinand was wishing her downstairs.

At dinner they sought refuge in abstractions. They talked

of dykes and windmills and cigars, the history of Holland and its constitution, the constitution of the United States and the edifying spectacle of the politics of that blessed country. They talked of political economy and pessimism and cattle rearing, the state of agriculture in England, the foreign policy of the day, Anarchism, the President of the French Republic. They would have talked of bi-metallism if they could. People hearing them would have thought them very learned and extraordinarily staid.

At last they separated, and as she undressed Valentia told herself that Ferdinand had kept his promise. Everything was just as it had been before, and the only change was that he used her Christian name. And she rather liked him to call her Valentia.

But next day Ferdinand did not seem able to command himself. When Valentia addressed him, he answered in monosyllables, with eyes averted; but when she had her back turned, she felt that he was looking at her. After breakfast she went away painting haystacks, and was late for luncheon.

She apologised.

'It is of no consequence,' he said, keeping his eyes on the ground. And those were the only words he spoke to her during the remainder of the day. Once, when he was looking at her surreptitiously, and she suddenly turned round, their eyes met, and for a moment he gazed straight at her, then walked away. She wished he would not look so sad. As she was going to bed, she held out her hand to him to say good-night, and she added,—

'I don't want to make you unhappy, Mr White. I'm very sorry.'

'It's not your fault,' he said. 'You can't help it, if you're a stock and a stone.'

He went away without taking the proffered hand. Valentia cried that night.

In the morning she found a note outside her door:—

'Pardon me if I was rude, but I was not master of myself. I am going to Volendam; I hate Monnickendam.'

VI

Ferdinand arrived at Volendam. It was a fishing village, only three miles across country from Monnickendam, but the route, by steam tram and canal, was so circuitous, that, with luggage, it took one two hours to get from place to place. He had walked over there with Valentia, and it had almost tempted them to desert Monnickendam. Ferdinand took a room at the hotel and walked out, trying to distract himself. The village consisted of a couple of score of houses, built round a semi-circular dyke against the sea, and in the semi-circle lay the fleet of fishing boats. Men and women were sitting at their doors mending nets. He looked at the fishermen, great, sturdy fellows, with rough, weather-beaten faces, huge earrings dangling from their ears. He took note of their quaint costume—black stockings and breeches, the latter more baggy than a Turk's, and the crushed strawberry of their high jackets, cut close to the body. He remembered how he had looked at them with Valentia, and the group of boys and men that she had sketched. He remembered how they walked along, peeping into the houses, where everything was spick and span, as only a Dutch cottage can be, with old Delft plates hanging on the walls, and pots and pans of polished brass. And he looked over the sea to the island of Marken, with its masts crowded together, like a forest without leaf or branch. Coming to the end of the little town he saw the church of Monnickendam, the red steeple half-hidden by the trees. He wondered where Valentia was—what she was doing.

But he turned back resolutely, and, going to his room, opened his books and began reading. He rubbed his eyes and frowned, in order to fix his attention, but the book said nothing but Valentia. At last he threw it aside and took his Plato and his dictionary, commencing to translate a difficult passage, word for word. But whenever he looked up a word he could only see Valentia, and he could not make head or tail of the Greek. He threw it aside also, and set out walking. He walked as hard as he could—away from Monnickendam.

The second day was not quite so difficult, and he read till his mind was dazed, and then he wrote letters home and told them he was enjoying himself tremendously, and he walked till he felt his legs dropping off.

Next morning it occurred to him that Valentia might have written. Trembling with excitement, he watched the postman coming down the street—but he had no letter for Ferdinand. There would be no more post that day.

But the next day Ferdinand felt sure there would be a letter for him; the postman passed by the hotel door without stopping. Ferdinand thought he should go mad. All day he walked up and down his room, thinking only of Valentia. Why did she not write?

The night fell and he could see from his window the moon shining over the clump of trees about Monnickendam church—he could stand it no longer. He put on his hat and walked across country; the three miles were endless; the church and the trees seemed to grow no nearer, and at last, when he thought himself close, he found he had a bay to walk round, and it appeared further away than ever.

He came to the mouth of the canal along which he and Valentia had so often walked. He looked about, but he could see no one. His heart beat as he approached the little bridge, but Valentia was not there. Of course she would not come out alone. He ran to the hotel and asked for her. They told him she was not in. He walked through the town; not a soul was to be seen. He came to the church; he walked round, and then—right at the edge of the trees—he saw a figure sitting on a bench.

She was dressed in the same flowered dress which she had worn when he likened her to a Dresden shepherdess; she was looking towards Volendam.

He went up to her silently. She sprang up with a little shriek.

'Ferdinand!'

'Oh, Valentia, I cannot help it. I could not remain away any longer. I could do nothing but think of you all day, all night. If you knew how I loved you! Oh, Valentia, have pity on me! I cannot be your friend. It's all nonsense about friendship; I hate it. I can only love you. I love you with all my heart and soul, Valentia.'

She was frightened.

'Oh! how can you stand there so coldly and watch my agony? Don't you see? How can you be so cold?'

'I am not cold, Ferdinand,' she said, trembling. 'Do you think I have been happy while you were away?'

'Valentia!'

'I thought of you, too, Ferdinand, all day, all night. And I longed for you to come back. I did not know till you went that—I loved you.'

'Oh, Valentia!'

He took her in his arms and pressed her passionately to him.

'No, for God's sake!'

She tore herself away. But again he took her in his arms, and this time he kissed her on the mouth. She tried to turn her face away.

'I shall kill myself, Ferdinand!'

'What do you mean?'

'In those long hours that I sat here looking towards you, I felt I loved you—I loved you as passionately as you said you loved me. But if you came back, and—anything happened—I swore that I would throw myself in the canal.'

He looked at her.

'I could not—live afterwards,' she said hoarsely. 'It would be too horrible. I should be—oh, I can't think of it!'

He took her in his arms again and kissed her.

'Have mercy on me!' she cried.

'You love me, Valentia.'

'Oh, it is nothing to you. Afterwards you will be just the same as before. Why cannot men love peacefully like women? I should be so happy to remain always as we are now, and never change. I tell you I shall kill myself.'

'I will do as you do, Valentia.'

'You?'

'If anything happens, Valentia,' he said gravely, 'we will go down to the canal together.'

She was horrified at the idea; but it fascinated her.

'I should like to die in your arms,' she said.

For the second time he bent down and took her hands and kissed them. Then she went alone into the silent church, and prayed.

VII

They went home. Ferdinand was so pleased to be at the hotel again, near her. His bed seemed so comfortable; he was so happy, and he slept, dreaming of Valentia.

The following night they went for their walk, arm in arm; and they came to the canal. From the bridge they looked at the water. It was very dark; they could not hear it flow.

No stars were reflected in it, and the trees by its side made the depth seem endless. Valentia shuddered. Perhaps in a little while their bodies would be lying deep down in the water. And they would be in one another's arms, and they would never be separated. Oh, what a price it was to pay! She looked tearfully at Ferdinand, but he was looking down at the darkness beneath them, and he was intensely grave.

And they wandered there by day and looked at the black reflection of the trees. And in the heat it seemed so cool and restful. . . .

They abandoned their work. What did pictures and books matter now? They sauntered about the meadows, along shady roads; they watched the black and white cows sleepily browsing, sometimes coming to the water's edge to drink, and looking at themselves, amazed. They saw the huge-limbed milkmaids come along with their little stools and their pails, deftly tying the cow's hind legs that it might not kick. And the steaming milk frothed into the pails and was poured into huge barrels, and as each cow was freed, she shook herself a little and recommenced to browse.

And they loved their life as they had never loved it before.

One evening they went again to the canal and looked at the water, but they seemed to have lost their emotions before it. They were no longer afraid. Ferdinand sat on the parapet and Valentia leaned against him. He bent his head so that his face might touch her hair. She looked at him and smiled, and she almost lifted her lips. He kissed them.

'Do you love me, Ferdinand?'

He gave the answer without words.

Their faces were touching now, and he was holding her hands. They were both very happy.

'You know, Ferdinand,' she whispered, 'we are very foolish.'

'I don't care.'

'Monsieur Rollo said that folly was the chief attribute of man.'

'What did he say of love?'

'I forget.'

Then, after a pause, he whispered in her ear,—

'I love you!'

And she held up her lips to him again.

'After all,' she said, 'we're only human beings. We can't help it. I think—'

She hesitated; what she was going to say had something of the anti-climax in it.

'I think—it would be very silly if—if we threw ourselves in the horrid canal.'

'Valentia, do you mean—?'

She smiled charmingly as she answered,—

'What you will, Ferdinand.'

Again he took both her hands, and, bending down, kissed them. . . . But this time she lifted him up to her and kissed him on the lips.

VIII

One night after dinner I told this story to my aunt.

'But why on earth didn't they get married?' she asked, when I had finished.

'Good Heavens!' I cried. 'It never occurred to me.'

'Well, I think they ought,' she said.

'Oh, I have no doubt they did. I expect they got on their bikes and rode off to the Consulate at Amsterdam there and then. I'm sure it would have been his first thought.'

'Of course, some girls are very queer,' said my aunt.

What is art fiction?

The intersection of art and life. Painting with words. Portmay Press brings contemporary and classic works of art fiction to a wide readership.

Other titles of interest from Portmay Press

Art Fiction Stories I
Edited by Genevieve Sheets

A Landscape Painter
Henry James

Printz
Maryann D'Agincourt

All Most
Maryann D'Agincourt

www.PortmayPress.com

www.ingramcontent.com/pod-product-compliance
Lightning Source LLC
LaVergne TN
LVHW050535100826
845148LV00002B/568